shirley marr

fury

black dog

First published in 2010 by
black dog books
15 Gertrude Street
Fitzroy Vic 3065 Australia
+61 3 9419 9406
+61 3 9419 1214 (fax)
dog@bdb.com.au
www.bdb.com.au

Shirley Marr asserts the moral right to be identified as author of this Work.

Cover design by Ellie Exarchos
Printed and bound in Australia by Griffin Press
Cover photograph © Pawel Piatek / Trevillion Images
Author photograph © Red Images Fine Photography

The paper in this book is sourced from Finland and manufactured under ISO 14001 certification from wood grown in certified forests.
No old-growth forest wood has been used in the manufacture of this book.

National Library of Australia Cataloguing-in-Publication data:
    Marr, Shirley
    Fury/Shirley Marr
    First edition
    ISBN (pbk.) 9781742031323
    For secondary school age
    A823.4

10 9 8 7 6 5 4 3 2 1   10 11 12 13 14 15

For D.N.F., for the graffiti you left on me.
And for everyone who has ever been Furious
because they had to be
and wanted to be
—S.M.

He sent his burning anger, rage, fury, and hostility against them.
He sent an army of destroying angels.
Psalm 78:49

one

My name is Eliza Boans and I am a murderer.

I *know*. It's pretty shocking, huh?

To think I actually had a better surname before my parents divorced and my mother went back to her maiden name, taking me kicking and screaming with her. See, the judge gave Dad the Jag and gave Mum, well, *me*. She spewed big time over that. But seriously, unlike what that do-gooder Chaplain here thinks, I didn't just wake up one morning and say to myself, "what a lovely day, I think I might go out and kill someone."

I'm the last person that anyone would have suspected. I'm just Lizzie, typical teenager. I'm all about angst, attitude, designer labels and cupcakes. I want to grow up and do something cool with my life, such as build an orphanage in a third world country like all those saintly Hollywood celebrities. That or, like, cause a scandal and become mega-famous. Everyone knows that's how you get noticed these days. I live in the suburbs, go to high school, and my mum has all these unrealistic expectations of how well I'm going to do in Year Twelve blah, blah, blah. The only difference between you and me is that I live in East Rivermoor.

A great wall runs all the way around our suburb. Access is through a double gate that has our own special crest on it. This is not just any neighbourhood; check your reality before you enter.

There is everything that you could possibly want here. The best shopping and heaps of trendy cafés, bars and restaurants that always get drool-worthy reviews in the magazines. A huge park in the middle with acres of rolled-on green lawn and a lake so large it has its own suspension bridge. You can keep your fancy yachts here; the water eventually takes you out into the ocean. Well-buffed guys practise rowing on weekends.

It's not a right to live here; it's a privilege. A privilege of being rich. There's no need to go outside these walls, if you don't want to.

I go to Priory Grammar of East Rivermoor, which everyone refers to by the one word: *Priory*. Makes it sound like a white monastery or a glass hospital. It's private, of course; as if it would be a public school. You need to, like, have money to live in East Rivermoor in the first place. Sure, we have scholarships for smart students from the povo suburbs, so you can get in if you're special and your parents aren't. But I don't know anyone here who has a parent below a doctor, lawyer, CEO or self-made entrepreneur.

At Priory, no expense has been spared for the offspring of the elite. No concrete landscaping or cyclone fencing here, unlike other schools I've only heard rumours of. Priory's been the top Tertiary Entrance Exam ranked school five years in a row. It's all beautiful and perfect. Even the girl's toilets smell like vanilla cake.

Don't get jealous just yet. Let me tell you my story first. It's *really* awful. Something worse than making a fool of yourself in front of the cute boy you've been eyeing all semester; much worse than showing up to the end-of-school ball in the same dress as the best looking chick in your grade. It's about a crime me and my best friends committed. No one thought that what I did could happen. Not in a safe place like East Rivermoor Not in a snobby, insufferable place like this.

I think you can tell by now that this is not going to be a happy story. If it were just some teenager's account of the last sunshine-filled days of high school, topped with a graduation and coming-of-age lesson at the end, then I wouldn't bother. You can go and read, like, *Snatcher in the Rye* or whatever, with the losers not doing English Lit.

The truth is we — me, Marianne, Lexi and Ella — never even made it to our graduation.

I heard that Isabella Hervey spiked the fruit punch and that Professor Adler snogged Miss Bailoutte behind the DJ booth. Like, *eww* old people. There was also reportedly a bitch fight on the dance floor involving the school football captain Richard Edwards, two admirers and a misdirected text message. What a shame we never got to see any of that for ourselves. Nobody signed our yearbooks. If we asked now, no one would want to.

The graduation song turned out to be *Extraordinary* by Mandy Moore. Fireworks exploded over everyone's heads as they made their way outside the school auditorium. It was a really touching moment, apparently. I guess the song wasn't intended for us. It doesn't matter: that song is crap.

Instead, the four of us spent what was supposed to be our graduation night locked in separate rooms at the police station in the city. We weren't allowed to see each other. They told us that we had done enough damage already. Maybe they thought that if they put us together we might kill each other. They already believe that we're capable of murdering somebody.

Ella's mother was the first to come, armed with huge bagfuls of food. She cried when that detective or whatever he is — Dr Fadden — told her she couldn't give them to her daughter. He told her that Ella deserved punishment. Mrs Dashwood sobbed and said that Ella was just a little girl.

Dr Fadden folded his arms. It said, silently, that he thought Ella was old enough.

Let's get one thing straight. I don't expect you to feel sorry for me. Hell, I don't think Mum does. That's why I'm not going to give her the chance to tell me how much I've failed her. I refuse to see her, or that woman-lawyer she's hired for me who specialises in "troubled" teenage girls. The only commitment I've seen them both demonstrate is trying to outdo each other in the short skirt department.

As for my dad, well, I don't have what you call an *active dad*. Not anymore. He walked out on us a long time ago and he never looked back. In fact, he took off so fast he's not even in the same country anymore. *Boohoo* you're probably thinking. *Poor little rich East Rivermoor girl*. Yeah, I should probably go and cry into my new Fendi handbag that Mum bought me. That might make me feel better.

They found the body Tuesday morning. A group of kids who walk to school along that way discovered it. I never meant for anything like that to happen. I mean, those kids were only in Year Eight. I'm really sorry that they'll probably have to be in therapy for the rest of their lives, but their parents should know better than to let them walk along the border of East Rivermoor to get to school. Beyond the border is the rest of the imperfect, dangerous world.

If I had known better I would have kicked that body and rolled it down that ditch. Then maybe it would have stayed there undisturbed until it rotted away to bone, and then from bone to dust. Right next to the billboard advertising what a wonderful place East Rivermoor is to live.

I'm not sorry I killed the person that body used to be.

They took Ella first, on the afternoon of that same Tuesday. She was at home freaking out. I guess she had reason to, considering how close the body was to her house. Then they came to take me, Lexi and Marianne.

We were all at my place studying for the English Lit final. They knew we were there; it was quite obvious who told them, *cough-that-snivelling-traitor-Ella-cough*. When I opened the door, the dried bloodstain I was wearing over my heart like a badge of honour told them, *these are the ones who did it*. When they got the cuffs out, it said, *these are the ones who deserve it*.

Mum wasn't there when they came to knock on the door. In fact, she hadn't been home for two weeks. I had no idea where she had gone or who she was with. Her very important work takes her places and she often has to jet off just like that. Well, now that she has finally rushed back, it's too late. I think that's fair enough for me to say. She was supposed to be there for me from the start. I know she'll be devastated that I'm going to miss my exams. Mum wanted to see me go to a good university, i.e., the one that she went to. I guess I'll just have to take the exams next year. That's if I'm allowed to. Do they let you sit the TEE if you're in jail?

Dr Fadden has made it clear that we will be going to a proper jail. We won't be going to some "cushy" juvey detention centre or some "rejuvenation" hospital by trying to pull an insanity plea. He says the law is going to come down hard, like, "you don't even know *how hard*". He says the law doesn't care if we are children; we have committed a very adult act and will thus be treated as adults.

I know the doctor thinks I am a spoilt brat. He doesn't need to tell me that; I know I am. As for his thinking that I need to be taught a lesson — I didn't think it was a crime to live in an expensive house, own sixty-five-and-counting pairs of shoes, have my own credit card and be promised a sports car when I get my licence. I know what lesson he really thinks I need to learn. I know guys like him: the ones that live on the other side of the wall. He doesn't know anything about me.

So let me introduce Dr Fadden. I thought I'd seen the end of him, after he spent last night grilling me. But this morning, to my horror, I find that he's the caseworker assigned to me. He's kind of hardened and mean, even though he looks young and reckons he is not technically a cop. He says he's an anthropologist. Maybe he thinks he can study the truth out of me. Maybe he's hoping that if he cracks this case and put us all away for life, he might get promoted to some cushy high-profile cop job. I am not sure how much money anthropologists make these days. Probably not a lot.

Since this *doctor* already knows I am guilty, his job is to find out to what extent. I take it the police have found more than one set of prints on the knife. So I'm going to try my hardest to hate him. I know that he's going to try and turn me against my friends so we get hysterical and point fingers, but I'm not interested in playing his games. I know better than that. After all, they say the apple doesn't drop far from the tree. And I just happen to be the daughter of the highest profile female lawyer in the state. The one they call *Bombshell Barrister Boans*.

◆❖

"Let's go over this again," says Dr Fadden. "Is there anything else you want to tell me, Eliza?"

I put my forehead down on the table.

"This is not helping," says Dr Fadden, unhelpfully.

We are seated in some really disgusting, dingy room. It has a metal table and chairs so old and ugly, I reckon even the residents of Middlemore would be too embarrassed to put them out as kerb collect. There's one of those fluoro-tube lights on the ceiling: the type that blink and make a humming noise. I have never seen a single building in East Rivermoor with one of those. I have to say that it does not impress me.

"Why are you interviewing me?" I ask. "Aren't you supposed to be an anthropologist? Shouldn't you be looking at the body instead of looking at me?"

"Lack of funding in the police department," replies Dr Fadden without skipping a beat. "Plus I've already looked at the body."

"Oh yeah?"

"Whoever was responsible for the stabbing plunged the

knife so hard into the chest, it pierced the rib cage. We found miniscule fragments of bone on the blade."

"Cheery," I reply.

"I work with live humans as well, if that helps answer your question."

I try to think of some derogatory names for him, but not a lot of words rhyme with Fadden and I give up at "Dr Fathead". But I know he's not just some dopey, doughnut-eating cop I can completely dismiss. I can see it in his eyes. They appear to be connected to a brain. Maybe he is mean to me because he thinks I am cruel.

Dr Fadden has what my mum would call a good Mediterranean complexion. His eyes turn slightly downwards at the corners, which give him a permanently sad look. I watch him from where my head still is, on the table with my cheek pressed against the cold metal. Maybe I will regret trying to play up when the side of my face breaks out in zits. I want to hate him. He's making it hard by being good-looking.

"Can I have a coffee?"

From my position I can see Dr Fadden's sideways face raise its eyebrows.

"I'm sixteen, not ten you know."

"I know," he replies. "I've read the police report. In fact, I've read your entire file and I probably know your life better than you do."

I pull my head back up.

"I've been drinking coffee since I was, like, thirteen,"

I say and try to sound mature. "And I've been sitting in cafés drinking frappucinos since I was maybe ten. It's — y'know — normal."

I can see him looking at the dirty school uniform I still have on, and my messed-up hair, and the blood as the words "We grow up pretty fast these days, trust me," come tumbling carelessly out of my mouth. And I know he is wondering.

"Okay." He shrugs and stands up.

"No!"

It comes out as a shout.

"I mean — *please*," I say and adjust my voice, "can I go with you and make it myself? I've been sitting here for hours doing *nothing*. I might get, like, mental damage. Pretty please?"

"May I remind you that this is not a five-star resort?" Dr Fadden says in his no-nonsense voice. "You have committed a very serious crime. I want you to take all of this seriously. For your own sake."

He doesn't have to tell me that. I know that this is *definitely* no five-star resort.

"I am," I reply and I do that thing where I make my eyes go real big. Perhaps I should also quiver my lip for effect.

The doctor sighs.

"Quickly then. And if anyone sees you, you're responsible for making up the excuse. Come on."

I don't move at first. I sit exactly where I am with my hands clenched between my knees.

"Out," he says firmly like he's talking to a dog, or like he's a man on a commercial ordering a beetroot stain off the collar of a white shirt.

I move.

Yes, I think silently, and in my head I do an arm-pump thing like a dumb-ass cheerleader. I know he's just trying to score brownie points with me, but I like Dr Fadden a bit better. He is young and impressionable. Maybe if I keep a tight leash on him he won't get the better of me. I learnt that trick from my mum.

Dr Fadden stands holding the door open. I smile at him as I squeeze eagerly past and hurry down the white hallway.

I hear his guarded, squeaky footsteps trailing behind.

"Slow down. Don't run in the hallway."

Ugh. Bad flashbacks. This is just like being back at Priory. He is as bad as snarky old Principal Hollerings.

"Can I see Lexi? What about Marianne?"

I reach the end of the hallway and turn to my left. I stumble into another too-bright, fluorescent-white room. I am still a little dazed when I realise I'm in a kitchen. And standing at the laminate bench with her back to me, is Ella.

"Oh my God!" I try to say, but it gets stuck halfway in my throat. I make a sort of gagging noise instead.

Ella spins around and her eyes widen.

"Oh Lizzie! Am I so happy to see you!"

I can't contain myself. I haven't seen Ella since we left the body and went our separate ways. She is quivering like a puppy. I walk up to her. Then I lunge at her throat.

That's when I find that something — or more precisely someone — is holding me back. It is Dr Fadden.

◆❖

I first met Ella over chicken cacciatore.

The night before, Mum had promised she would make me lunch for the first day back at school after term break. *Yes*, I know I can make my own sandwich. I mean, how hard is it to slap two pieces of bread together? But like I've already told you, I'm lazy and spoilt.

In the morning I opened the fridge door to find no brown paper lunchbag containing my favourite chicken and Jarlsberg cheese on rye. Instead, inside the fridge, between the bottle of red wine and the bottle of white, lay a flat twenty-dollar note.

That was how I found myself in the hot canteen queue, along with all the other kids with busy or lazy parents. I piled some of the canteen slop on my plate without looking. Everything was covered in the same identical cheese, and I watched as it melted and made a goopy lump on the communal serving spoon. *So* disgusting. You would think this was prison. Or a public high school.

To my left, an unfamiliar girl slid next to me along the self-serve counter and grabbed a plate. I guess I mustn't have noticed her standing behind me in the queue. For good reason too. Average height. Average weight. Average brown hair. Average length on that average brown hair. I lost interest and concentrated on trying to flick cheese strings back into the bainmarie.

"Chicken thingy…beef thingy…fish thingy…vegetable thingy…*thing* thingy," the girl recited to herself as she inspected each sauce-flecked label. She took a small scoop of each and arranged it onto her plate so none of them touched the other.

Okay, I was intrigued. I looked at my own plate, where I had made some sort of sloppy, cheesy mountain.

"Eliza Boans," I said and held out my free hand.

"Oh, hi. Ellanoir Dashwood. Call me Ella," she said animatedly and shook my hand. "This is my first day at Priory. Isn't it great? Look at this dining hall, doesn't it look beautiful? Like a palace…not that I have ever been in a palace myself, but it's what I imagine a dining hall in a palace would look like…"

"Um, yeah," I replied as I hurried ahead. "Hope you, er… enjoy it here. See you around then, I guess."

I wondered which planet Ellanoir Dashwood had just landed from.

◆❖

"What? People pay that much to eat this crap?" I said to Mrs Wally, Wes' mum, at the cash register.

Yes, that's right. Her son, our school debating champion, is called *Wes Wally*. Some people must think the miracle of birth is hilarious. Especially Mrs Wally. Everyone knows she has no class anyway. She may be rich now, with her geriatric, mining-king husband, but we all know which side of the wall she came from. It shows too, from her giant hoop earrings down to her gum chewing and pink velour tracksuits. I heard that Mrs Wally was working here on community service for drink driving. Apparently she drove her Mercedes over a roundabout instead of going around it. Only problem was that she didn't expect to be unceremoniously stopped by the palm tree in the middle.

"Watch your language, Miss Eliza, or I may be forced to report you," said Mrs Wally, trying unsuccessfully to frown with her botoxed-up forehead. "Now pay up and move along. You're holding up the queue."

I scowled and un-scrunched the twenty-dollar note out of my new Belle Bijoux coin purse. "Whatever. Here, take it. Actually, just keep the whole lot. I don't need it."

I attempted to flick the note like a ninja star, but unfortunately my cool manoeuvre did not execute well, and I literally pelted the money at her. I grabbed my plastic tray and marched off. She used to waitress in a Middlemoore sushi bar before she struck gold; I'm sure she's used to rude customers. She can consider the rest of the twenty a tip.

I walked quickly, scanning the lunch-hall, and spied Lexi and Marianne sitting on a bench in the corner by a large potted palm. I stuck my hand up and waved just as Justin Hawkins ran past and smacked a scrunched-up paper napkin at me. It had something sticky on it that clung to my hair.

Loser! I wanted to shout. But I held my tongue. The hall was too loud anyway and I guess I didn't want everyone to stare at me. I put my head down and beelined quickly toward Lexi and Marianne.

"Forget your lunch today?" said Marianne.

"There's something gross in your hair," said Lexi.

"I know and *I know*," I replied and dropped my tray down. "Don't remind me, please."

I looked at the both of them, sitting quietly and almost expressionless.

One is blonde and just back from a yachting holiday in the Greek Islands. She's got the Goldilocks of tans; it's just right. Not too pale and not too tanorexic.

The other one is brunette with skin so white that if she were any paler, she would be, like, Nicole Kidman.

"Justin Hawkins is such an immature little brat," drawled Marianne, my blonde friend, as if the idea of Justin Hawkins being a brat bored her. She was delicately eating a white bread sandwich wrapped in greaseproof paper. I could smell the smoked chicken, baby spinach and vintage cheddar. I was jealous.

"Here. Let me fix that," said Lexi, and she got up to seat herself next to me.

"Eliza! You move so fast! I was trying to keep up."

The small figure of Ella loomed terrifyingly close, clutching her tray. The food on her plate was still perfectly separated.

"Oh. Hi again. Um, sit down. Lexi and Marianne,

this is Ella. She's new. Ella — *vice versa*."

"Hi Vice and hallo Versa!" quipped Ella.

I watched the faces of my two friends to see their reactions. There were none.

Ella plonked her tray down and stretched her hand across the table toward Marianne.

"Ellanoir Dashwood."

Marianne looked back at her calmly.

"As in Jane Austen?"

"No, not *Elinor*! It's *Ella-noir*. Although actually, that's exactly where my mum got my name from — *Sense & Sensibility*. She thought Ellanoir would be, I guess, classier."

"Oh I see, *Ella-nywar*," said Marianne holding out her hand. "How do you do, Ella-*nywar*?"

Ella squeezed herself down on the bench beside me. Lexi eyed Ella curiously.

Marianne stared at us, and I caught her passing a "blink-and-miss" look to Lexi. I didn't miss it. I knew it was a signal. Lexi looked at her, acknowledged and then looked away.

I didn't miss that either.

"I'm still new to this suburb. East Rivermoor." Ella sighed loudly when she said East Rivermoor Like she was talking about somewhere romantic and perched on a cloud in rainbow land.

"My mum and I just moved in last week. We came from…um actually, that's probably not important. But, East Rivermoor, it's so — nice!"

"Nice?" repeated Marianne. "Yeah, I suppose so…"

"We've moved into the purple house. You know the one that looks kinda white-washed? But it's not white. It's purple. Like aubergine. Aubergine-washed? And it has a roof that looks kinda like waffles."

"Actually, no." Marianne replied bluntly and shifted her eyes in my direction. "Just like none of the houses in East Rivermoor are made of gingerbread, I don't know any aubergine and waffle house…"

"I do."

I glared back at Marianne. "It's a few streets down from my place. You should know which house Ella is talking about. I'm ashamed of you, Marianne. I thought your family was one of the oldest in East Rivermoor."

Marianne averted her eyes.

"I live in the blue house on The Bourne, Ella. And Lexi lives just around the corner from me."

Ella made a sudden high-pitched noise like a small chihuahua.

"What? Are you *serious*? You're totally kidding me! The blue house? With the three levels and the white trims? With the *turret*? You honestly live there? That is just, like, the best house in East Rivermoor. Can I come over some time?"

"Sure," I replied. I guess I didn't have much choice. I was trying to prove a point to Marianne, even though I didn't really know what my point was.

Marianne groaned. I kicked her under the table. She

yelped loudly, but I ignored her and took a mouthful of my disgusting cheese mountain.

"Ugh. Revolting!"

"The chicken cacciatore is not altogether that bad," said Ella happily, stabbing her fork into a cube of something that did not look like chicken.

I looked down at my unrecognisable pile. I swore something deep inside of it quivered in anticipation of being eaten. Lexi had finished cleaning the gunk out of my hair and was unwrapping her own lunch. I couldn't tell you how badly I wanted Lexi's lunch — a poppy seed bagel with smoked salmon, dill and cream cheese.

"You know what I think? Only the kids whose parents don't care enough about them subject them to the canteen lunch," piped Marianne out of the blue.

She turned toward Lexi who said nothing. I fumed and wanted to glare at her, but she just smiled serenely down at her own perfectly half-eaten sandwich.

"Ella, what do you have next class?" I asked loudly.

"Um…History in Room N14, I think…"

"Excellent. So do I." I dropped my fork and stood up.

"On second thoughts, I'm not hungry. Ella and I are going to go to class early. So I can show Ella…stuff."

I glared at both of them and pushed my plate so it came to rest between the two of them. "Here, have a nice little chat over this. I don't care. *Whatever.* Seeya. "

I threw my satchel over my shoulder and grabbed Ella's

arm, extracting her from the bench mid-mouthful and away from my two so-called *friends*.

"Marianne and Lexi are…nice," said Ella, puffing. I realised we were almost running.

"You think so?" I replied sarcastically.

I slowed down. They re-tiled all the hallways in Italian porcelain during the semester break. I guess Principal Hollerings wanted everyone breaking the rules to slip and break their necks. That would definitely teach the naughty children not to run through the corridors.

"They don't say much, I have to admit. But they really are so pretty," replied Ella. "I've never sat at a table with girls like that before…I guess it's always been a dream of mine, you know, like in those books about girls and boarding schools…"

"Enjoy the novelty while it lasts, honey," I replied and I steered her toward the South Wing.

The South Wing was unveiled just this morning during our boring welcome back this-is-the-last-term-before-the-TEE-so-be-good-and-for-godsakes-behave assembly. It used to be the old East Rivermoor Powerhouse so it's, like, a hundred years old. The museum wanted to move here, but Priory is richer than the government, so it's become our new History, Arts and Social Studies wing. It cost millions, apparently. But hey, it's just money. This is our education we're talking about.

◆❖

We arrived fifteen minutes early for Mr Carter's class. I found myself lowering my head a little as we stood in the corridor outside. I didn't want to appear desperate, with a new girl with me and everything. It's hard just surviving high school sometimes; trying to balance being eager, but not *that* eager. Pity really, because I like History. I mean, I wish there weren't so many boring dates and facts to remember, but I really like all the stuff to do with scandals and murders and assassinations. Did Anastasia of the Royal Russian family actually survive the execution of her entire family? Did Lee Harvey Oswald really kill John F. Kennedy? Did you know that Anne Boleyn wore a red and grey damask gown to her beheading — what a total fashion-babe. And I actually like Mr Carter. He never pads out a class just to stretch it to the full hour. If we finish early he lets us watch music videos.

Mr Carter was also early for class. To be honest, I don't think he's super old, not like, *forty*, but he dresses like he's just stepped out of the poor little wardrobe that time forgot. But vintage is cool; it's the new black. Mr Carter indicated that we should enter the classroom first, so we trundled in awkwardly before him. He's a gentleman like that.

"I see we have a new pupil, Miss Boans, unless you are chaperoning her around for your own entertainment?"

"Er, yes we do and no I'm not," I replied.

"Then, pray introduce us."

"Oh," I said and I felt myself blushing. "This is Ella. I mean, Ellanoir."

"Ellanoir?" repeated Mr Carter. He pronounced "noir" properly in a European accent. Not in a Middlemoore bogan accent like Marianne.

"Ellanoir Dashwood," Ella blurted.

Then she did something that I have never, ever seen anyone do before in real life. She curtsied.

"Miss Dashwood," said Mr Carter and a smile played across his face. "Delighted. Please have a seat with Eliza."

"Let's be backseat bandits," I whispered to Ella.

"Huh?"

"It just means we don't sit right up the front — oh, never mind, let's just sit here."

From the corner of my eye I could see Mr Carter smiling at us. He's actually pretty hot for someone his age.

"What was that?" I whispered as we plonked ourselves down.

"What?"

"*That*." I inclined my head and lifted an imaginary skirt.

"Oh! Sorry. That was a…nervous twitch. I don't normally do *that*. I hope *you* don't think I normally do that! I swear. I promise it won't happen again."

She was definitely a strange one. But I kinda liked that. She's quirky. Quirky is cool: it's like the new…er…*new*…

More students started arriving noisily from outside and Mr Carter welcomed them in with a lazy wave of his hand. He strode down the middle of the room between the desks, snatching a comic book off Daniel Smalls as he passed.

"Early once again, Boans?" snarled Smalls under his breath.

"Well you're not exactly...late yourself!" I snapped back.

Oh my God, how lame was that?

Smalls snickered and I hid the side of my face with my palm.

"Miss Boans!"

Mr Carter's voice echoed from somewhere beyond the classroom door.

"Was that your voice I just heard heckling your fellow students?"

Daniel Smalls looked back in my direction and a smirk broke out across his hamster cheeks. Looked like he'd gotten himself a new buzz cut during the break. He really should do us all a favour and go ahead and join the army.

"That is so unfair!" I turned to Ella and muttered. "How can Mr C. blame me? Didn't he even hear Smalls?"

I craned my neck to see Mr Carter standing just outside the door, talking to two almost identical-looking students. *Identical* as in they were both blonde, sported the same haircut and were wearing their school uniform in exactly the same way. *Almost*, as in one was tall, thin and good-looking. The other was short, tubby and rather...fugly.

I grabbed Ella's shoulder. "Hey, look."

Ella turned eagerly in the same direction.

"See those girls? You'll never see one without the other.

They even chose the same subjects so they can take all their classes together. They aren't twins, but they might as well be. They're both called Jane. We call them the *Jane Blondes*."

I laughed at my own joke.

Ella stared for the longest time.

"Who is 'we'?"

"Lexi, Marianne and me of course."

Ella stared again at the Jane Blondes.

"That is sort of mean," she said finally. "They are so beautiful."

"They are *not* beautiful. They're pure nastiness. Look, you don't know anything about them, not like we do. Last weekend I had on this white dress, and we bumped into them at the Leftbank and one of them had a bright blue slushie…"

But Ella wasn't listening anymore. She was unpacking the contents of her pencil case instead. She had a large Japanese eraser in the shape of a panda, with three tiny baby ones in the shapes of a penguin, dolphin and a sunfish. She was lining them up across the desk.

A thin shape suddenly cast a dark shadow in front of us.

"New girl, eh? What's your name, new girl?"

I looked up to find Jeremy Biggins standing in front of us. Ella slowly looked up as well. I could see Biggins' sidekick, Smalls, leering again in our direction.

"My name's Ella. Who are you?"

"Biggins is my name. Jeremy Biggins. So *Ella-ella-ella,* you reckon you…fancy this *fella*?"

"Huh?" said Ella.

"Don't say anything," I said.

"*Ella* won't you be my…*Cinderella*?"

Biggins put his grimy paws onto the edges of our desks.

"Wouldn't you like some of my…*mortadella*?"

From the corner of my eye I could see Smalls double-up in laughter. That was enough. I stiffened my hand and chopped right into Jeremy Biggins' wrist.

"*Oww*!" yelped Biggins and he released both his hands from the desks. I couldn't tell what was reddening faster: Biggins' wrist or his cheeks.

"Good," I said. "I hope I broke something."

"Why you horrible little…"

I stood up. I was half-a-head taller than Biggins.

"That will teach you to shoot your mouth off! And you can tell your friend over there to shut up as well! I don't know why you are called Biggins when you are actually quite small. Especially when your friend Smalls is, funnily enough, quite big. Come on, Ella."

I dragged her from her chair and up the middle of the room towards the door. Ella protested the entire way.

"You'll get into trouble for assaulting another student, Boans!" yelled Biggins.

"Don't tell me you didn't have it coming!" I shouted back.

It was unfortunate that I happened to shout this right into Mr Carter's ear.

"Excuse me, Miss Boans?" Mr Carter asked, shocked.

"Ask him!" I said angrily. Before he could say anything I pushed Ella out the door and we both scampered away. In fact, Ella didn't seem to need any encouragement. I had to keep up with her as she ran half a length in front of me up the South corridor, forgetting about the new Italian tiles. Mr Carter stared after us, speechless. He hurriedly tried to usher the Janes into class, but not before I could feel their cold blue eyes boring into the back of my head.

They say that all daughters eventually grow up to become their mothers. I totally detest my mother, but I am trying to accept my Fate. I have realised that I am hot-tempered, unreasonable and I do stupid, impulsive things…just like my mother.

"Are you all right?" I asked Ella as I caught up to her.

"Of course I'm not!" She spat back.

She was rattling the glass door at the end of the hallway, trying to pull it open.

"Hey! Don't worry about Smalls and Biggins; they're idiots and they're always like that. If I had my way I'd—"

"I am not worried about them!"

"What do you mean?"

"I mean I can't believe that you just embarrassed me like

that in front of the whole class! On my first day at a respectable school and everything. Can you imagine what everyone must think of me?"

"Oh," I replied, staring at her angry, pinking face as she tugged at the door handle.

I wanted to tell Ella that just because the school was respectable didn't mean all the students were. Instead, I took hold of the handle and pushed the door outward. Ella pitched forward and almost landed on her face.

"You know, I *was* trying to help."

I followed Ella as she rushed out the door. The sudden brightness of the outside world hurt my eyes and I put out my arm to shade my face.

There were purple and red clouds that looked like smudges of bruise and blood against the face of the sky. Must be an electrical storm blowing in from the coast. I could feel the cool spring breeze in the air, flirting with my hair. I couldn't wait for summer.

Ella stomped down towards the school lake. It is not a real lake. It is as man-made and fake as the rest of East Rivermoor. She reached the old ghost-gum tree and threw herself on the grass. I sat down beside her.

"I didn't mean to cause a scene with you in it."

Ella said nothing. She pulled a dandelion out of the grass.

"I'm so sorry."

She beheaded the flower with her thumbnail and threw it over her shoulder.

"Is there anything I can do to make it up to you?"

Ella shook her head.

"Well, I'm sorry things turned out the way they did. It's not what I wanted either." I said, as nicely as I could. "Why don't we pretend that none of this ever happened and start from the beginning? You can pick who you want to be your friends over again. I mean, I promise I won't even look your way in the lunch-hall."

I smiled at Ella. She didn't smile back.

"Oh well. I don't know what to do now. I can't go back. So I reckon I'm just going to go home."

I stood up and started walking, dusting grass clippings off my backside.

"Wait," called Ella.

"Yeah?" I said and turned around.

"Are you still keeping your word that I can come over to see your house?"

"Um, yeah. If you still want to."

"I'd love to."

Ella stood up eagerly. "Our bags and things are still back at History class though."

I shrugged. "Doesn't really matter. I don't think anyone will touch them. I mean, who wants to pinch another copy of *Modern History*?"

For a split second I thought about Ella's primary school-like erasers. One large panda with three of its smaller friends all lined up. Where were they heading? I wondered if someone had knocked them off the desk already. After the cleaners had been, they'd probably be hoovered up and gone completely.

What a silly thing to think. I didn't even know why I thought it, so I forgot about it.

Ella smiled then. I held out my arm and she linked hers with mine.

◆❖

"Let go of me!" She screams again.

"Stop it," Dr Fadden says loudly into my ear. "Don't you think you are in enough trouble already?"

I stop struggling. Dr Fadden somehow manages to lift and turn me around in the other direction so I can't see Ella anymore.

"I hope you're happy with yourself, Ella!" I yell since I know she can still hear me.

"This is not what I wanted either, Lizzie!" Ella's voice wails back.

"Don't *Lizzie* me: I am not your Lizzie anymore! I don't think so, not after Lexi and Marianne were so kind to you and all you did was throw it back in their faces!"

"Don't make me sound like some charity case," whines Ella. "You were never my friends. You just felt sorry for me! Because I'm not a real Priory girl. Not like you three snobs!"

"You're right, you're not a charity case, 'cos a charity case would be grateful. You're a user!"

"Ellanoir?"

It is the voice of Ella's mum. She is standing in the doorway in front of me, wringing a handkerchief in her hands. Even in public she is wearing a Jane Austen dress. With her hair in a bun as severe as a librarian's.

"Dearest, come on. We're going home," she says, quickly gliding past the spectacle of me and Dr Fadden spooned in a one-way embrace.

I can hear Ella wipe her snot away and shuffle obediently toward her mother. There is silence for a few seconds. I take it they are having a hug. *Touching.*

Mrs Dashwood tows Ella along past me, her hand clasped tightly on top of her daughter's.

Ella, *forever-the-follower*. Jeremy Biggins didn't pick that one. He should have.

"You!" Mrs Dashwood stops and points her finger at me.

"How dare you do this to my daughter! I should have known better than to move to this neighbourhood. Just because you people are rich, doesn't mean you are any more civilised!"

Well no shit Sherlock. I could have told her that from the start and spared her the pain.

"We opened up our home to you and this is how you repay us? You are absolutely shameless. You are the most loathsome girl I have ever met! I hope you rot in jail. Ella, come, now!"

Ella whines the entire length of the room. Even after they have gone I can still hear her high-pitched voice bouncing off the corridor walls outside.

I suddenly realise that I am sliding downwards. My shoulders have inexplicably become weak and Dr Fadden is desperately trying to hold me up. Maybe my shoulders just don't work anymore, which is strange because I do Yogalates three times a week. Maybe I am giving up. I don't really know. I look up at the doctor.

"I want to go," I whisper.

Not that I have anywhere to go. I wonder what I mean, myself.

two

I must have been staring at this blank wall for ages. For the longest time, it's the only thing existing in my world. I am not aware of walking back into the interview room and sitting down on the hard metal chair. Or of Dr Fadden going out and then coming back again. All I feel is something hot suddenly shoved into my hands. It is a mug of steaming black coffee. I take a mouthful gratefully. Then I spit it back out when it burns the roof of my mouth.

"Back to square one," says Dr Fadden without a hint of irony. "And so are the days of our lives…"

I stare at the doctor. Slowly his features stop being just a set of shapes and lines and settle into a face again.

"Why is Ella allowed to leave?" I find my mouth moves itself to form the words. "What did she say? Have Marianne and Lexi gone too?"

"Well I guess Ella must have been a good girl and told the truth. Now, do you think it's fair that she gets to go and you're still sitting here?"

I scowl. "I am not loathsome. Mrs Dashwood doesn't know the first thing about me. I mean, I can be a good person too… "

Dr Fadden leans in closer to me across the table.

"Why don't you start then by telling me your side of the story?"

I lean in close to the middle of the table as well.

"No," I say.

"Oh," he replies.

"You see, unlike Ella, I'm going to stand up for my friends. Ella doesn't know the first thing about loyalty. You know what? I *don't* deserve to rot in jail! How can an adult even say something like that? To a sixteen-year-old as well! To someone as young and impressionable as me… "

"Eliza," says Dr Fadden. "*Earth to Planet Eliza.* Do you hear me all the way up there on your soapbox? All the more to prove them wrong, don't you see?"

I put my coffee down on the table. I place it so it is
perfectly spaced between Dr Fadden and me. It stands as
a small cylindrical barrier between us.

"Do I look like I'm stupid?" I say. "You fetching me this
coffee and suddenly becoming my Agony Uncle, when for
how long — weeks? Months? No one, *not one single person*,
has bothered to listen to me — to *us*! How do I even know
you didn't set up that whole thing in the kitchen before? To
try and get me to spill my guts?"

"Hey," replies Dr Fadden. "If I recall correctly, you were
the one who asked to be let out. I didn't ask you to stumble
across your friend and try to pull her hair out."

He sounds defensive. I open my mouth, but then I close it
again.

"I am only trying to help you, Eliza. If you don't talk to
me, how am I supposed to help?"

"Trust me, I — all of us — did a lot of talking. Do you
think it helped? If it did, then you tell me why am I sitting
here right now? I am done 'talking'. Period."

Dr Fadden sighs.

"Well, then I guess you'll end up like Ella's mum said. In
jail and forgotten. Ella gets to go home. To a hot bath and
a change of clothes, back to her comfortable room and bed.
To carry on with her normal life. To forget about you and
your friends."

Dr Fadden leans back on his chair and tips the front
legs up.

"Eventually she'll go to uni. Maybe she'll get the job she always dreamed of. Move out of home, meet a nice boy, get married, have children. And one day in the future, maybe she'll think, 'Oh, I wonder what happened to Eliza Boans, that girl I went to school with?' Or maybe she won't. Either way, you'd still be forgotten. So, what choice do you have, but to trust me?"

He pauses and waits for my reaction.

"Screw you," I reply.

Dr Fadden raises his eyebrows and uncrosses his arms. I do the same thing.

"*Trust* you? How can I trust you? I don't know who you are. I don't even know your first name."

He studies me with his fingers cupped in front of his mouth.

"It's Brian."

"See?" I point out, "I knew you'd never...*oh*."

We stare at each other. "Nice name."

I know a Brian from class and he's both a nerd and a creep at the same time; he will probably grow up to afford a beautiful mansion on The Bourne where he can build his own lovely torture dungeon.

"You lie," Dr Fadden says. "Brian is a terrible name. I know you think so: I can see it in your eyes."

He is studying me. For a moment I believe he can see right through me.

"When I was your age," continues Dr Fadden, "I wore

huge wire-framed glasses. I was a geek. The other kids called me *Brain*."

I force a smile. I don't know anyone who says *geek* anymore. And why is he telling me these things? Is he trying to win me over with his empathy? 'Cos I sure as hell can't relate to him.

I stare back at Dr Fadden. He is not wearing glasses of any description. He is good-looking. He doesn't look like a *geek*. But he could be a liar. I know better these days than to trust the cute boys.

"You say that you can't trust me, Eliza, but I probably have more trouble trusting you: have you ever thought about that?"

I say nothing.

"Why don't you tell me about Alexandria?"

Dr Fadden flicks something out of his manila folder and pushes it toward me. It is a picture of Lexi.

Lexi is, IMHO, the most beautiful girl at school. Jane Ayres of the Jane Blondes may be leggy and thin and blue-eyed, but she is as one-dimensional and fake as her bleached hair. Lexi looks like one of those laced-up heroines on the cover of the romance paperbacks my mother reads. *Three-for-the-price-of-two* at the airport, my mother's second home.

In the photo that Dr Fadden has out in front of me, Lexi looks like a cocaine whore.

When we were unceremoniously shipped to the police station yesterday, the first thing they did, after tearing us apart, was to take our photos. I wonder, if right at this moment, in another interrogation room, some other cop is showing Lexi my photo. I'll hate to know how I look in it.

That is, if Lexi is still here. Not sold out and gone too.

◆❖

I walked to school with Lexi as usual the morning after we first met Ella. I hate having to walk. *Anywhere.* I reckon one day when I get my licence and my mum gets me that Saab she promised, I will drive everywhere. Even to the corner deli to pick up my milk. Lexi, on the other hand, loves to walk. She was on a self-confessed "Jane Austen Exercise Program".

"Have you ever heard of any of her heroines being described as overweight? Never! And did they have treadmills and stepping machines back in those days? They stayed in shape because they lived hundreds of miles apart from each other so they had to walk everywhere." Lexi was all arms and hand gestures. "I have never been inside a gym and I never plan to, thank you very much. Gyms are so, like, Greco-homo-erotic."

I wouldn't say that Lexi's the skinniest girl I know, but she wasn't fat either, so maybe her exercise regime was working. Or maybe it's more like Lexi only eats one meal a day, except for on Mondays and Fridays, and has what she calls a "mild eating disorder".

I don't really mind walking with Lexi. She's always so chatty that it makes it easy when you have nothing good to say.

The streets here are very small and are for private vehicles only. They're paved with these pretty, dark-grey cobblestones in small rainbow patterns. We even have those old-fashioned lampposts ordered directly from London. I can't imagine how it must feel to live in a suburb with trucks and heavy traffic. The parents who live in places like that really should do better by their children.

Lexi carried her shoulder bag with one hand on the strap. Her fingernails were painted black. I didn't carry my school bag because it happened to still be in Mr Carter's classroom. My mother left me another twenty in the fridge, but Lexi had been sweet and made me a sandwich. She'd tied the paper bag with raffia, and had decorated it with a paper heart, my name handwritten neatly in the middle. Lexi doesn't have a mother so sometimes she becomes mine.

"I still like making lunch, even though I don't eat it," said Lexi, proud about both.

I rolled my eyes. Lexi makes out like she never eats, but I saw her tucking into that bagel yesterday and no doubt today she'll whip out another "I-packed-it-just-in-case-my-blood-sugar-levels-bottom-out lunch".

"Thanks, you're such a sweetheart," I replied.

I thought about leaving the twenty dollars in the fridge that morning just to spite Mum. Then I thought about how much I needed a new mascara, and with my credit card maxed out and all...I quickly shoved the note into my blazer before I changed my mind.

"So has your new BFF Ella been over yet to see the 'best house in East Rivermoor'?"

"Yes, *our* new friend Ella did come over after school yesterday. We walked home together."

"And?"

"She loved it. She was like, 'oh my God you have a powder room,' and I was like, 'we have four, actually,' and she almost peed herself. I think when I showed her my bedroom in the turret and my four-poster bed — that's when she truly died."

Lexi smiled wryly. "I realise I was kinda mean to Ella yesterday when I just sat there and said nothing…but like Marianne says, we can't let someone into our group just like that. We don't know anything about her."

"Since when have you listened to Marianne?" I replied and shot her a stony glance. Lexi looked away quickly.

"You know what I mean, Lizzie. We've known each other forever. Our parents have always known each other. You met Ella randomly in the lunch queue just yesterday."

"I know, but—"

"All I'm saying is that Marianne might be right. You said Ella's mother used to home-school her before they moved to East Rivermoor, right? Her mother could be some sort of freaky hermit. And anyway, this is our last term. We should just enjoy it together. Just the three of us."

I didn't reply. The Marianne thing got to me more than I would admit.

"Let's just let her hang around," I said finally. "She's

actually quite funny and quirky and pretty too. Okay, so we can work on the pretty part. The question is, do you want to see her fall into the hands of the Jane Blondes instead?"

"I guess not," replied Lexi, not sounding very convinced. "You're the boss after all. Oh. Hi."

A tall blond boy with black eyes slid up next to Lexi. Have you ever wondered where all the emo kids disappear to when the sun comes out? Well, some of them change out of their skinny jeans and go play sport. This was one of them. I called him by his last name, Aardant. Lexi called him by his first name, Alistair, and it made her blush every time.

"I heard the date has been set for the end-of-school ball," he said.

"Oh really?" replied Lexi and she started fiddling with her hair.

"I heard about it yesterday after training."

What a jerk. As if he didn't have a girlfriend already. And speaking of the she-devil, that girlfriend happened to be Jane Ayres. I wouldn't blame him for wanting to take Lexi to the ball instead of that psycho, but…

I flashed him a look and decided to walk ahead. I didn't want to hear him tell Lexi to check out those calves just made for slow dancing. For the first time in my life, I breathed a sigh of relief as I reached the school gates.

Somewhere along the line, the Parent and School Committee had decided that the air of sophistication Priory needed was a pair of golden gates, with cupids and cornucopias on top of them. The only problem was that the Parent and School Committee didn't want to appear cheap by getting gold leaf, so they got solid gold. As a result the gates are so heavy that they now remain permanently open. Doing an awesome job of keeping strangers out and truants in.

Unfortunately, standing at the open gate was the large figure of Daniel Smalls. I sucked in my breath.

"Boans!" He bellowed and pointed at me with his hand in the shape of a gun. "Hollerings wants to see you. You're in trouble — big time."

He shot his imaginary gun at me and sauntered off.

I scowled. I swear he's part troll. I've seen his father once and he looks just like a Ukrainian weightlifter.

"Thanks for the personal service!" I shouted at Smalls' retreating figure.

"Do you want me to come with you?" Lexi stood behind me, alone now.

"No…I'll go myself," I fumbled.

"Come on," said Lexi and she put her slender hand with its beautiful black-polished nails into the crook of my arm.

Lexi's a real humanitarian. She's beautiful and kind. She collected five thousand Coke can ring-pulls last year so that some missionary in Indonesia could make legs for land mine victims. She was so going to be Belle of the Ball this year.

I didn't want to go to Principal Hollerings' office. It's in the gross part of the school that's made of brown brick and brown panelling and well — brown everything. But when he moves into the new building, he will have the office befitting a Principal of Priory. It will have a grand entrance, a tropical atrium, a library antechamber and a reception foyer. Getting through to Principal Hollerings after that will be like trying to crack *The Da Vinci Code*.

Even though the first class of the day hadn't even started, I was not the first to the Principal's office. Shane McGowan was sitting on the bench, and Pete Noble was sitting on the other end, as far away from him as possible. They both had matching bruises on their faces. They both looked in opposite directions.

"Wow," I said to Pete. "How on earth did I miss out on getting a ticket? If I knew I would have been there ringside."

"Don't stress, Eliza," he smirked. "You can still come backstage."

They really should do something about the number of smart-asses being sent to the principal. You'd think that we were living in 1984, 'cos apparently back then they had a police state where everyone had the right to dob in everyone else. Kinda like this school system.

Stan Collymore and Paul Merson and the usual goon squad were also there. And so was Neil Fernandes.

During the term break, I'd received a postcard stamped

Dallas, Texas. From the Sixth Floor Assassination Museum, where you can check out the actual window that Lee Harvey Oswald shot JFK. It was signed: *you know who* and a smiley face. I could feel the postcard now, inside the pocket of my blazer. I was reminded it was there every time my heart beat.

Neil was leaning against the wall with his hands in his pockets.

I wanted to ask him if it was true that everyone in Texas wore huge shoulder pads and had big hair, but then he caught my eye and smiled. I pretended I didn't see him.

"*Neil!*" shouted Lexi.

"*Alex!*" replied Neil in the same tone.

"What did you do this time?"

"I locked Frank Bruno in the cleaners' cupboard after school yesterday."

"You did *what*?"

"It's all good. The cleaners found him this morning. I caught him trying to flush a Year Eight boy down the toilet. Thought he needed somewhere private to think about his actions. What did *you* do?"

Lexi pointed at me. "I'm just with this one."

"I always knew the quiet ones were trouble."

I frowned at Neil and opened my mouth to say something, but the Principal's door flew open.

"Miss Boans!" called a raspy voice.

"Hey, no fair, why do you get to go before me?" said Neil. "I've been in the queue for ages."

"'Cos she's special,' replied Lexi and she gave me an unhelpful push toward the door. "Ladies first."

◆❖

Principal Hollerings' office is exactly like his personality: without sentiment. There wasn't a single framed photo or personal touch that indicated what his interests or hobbies might be. If he had any at all. The only thing on his desk was a tray labelled OUT with nothing in it and a tray labelled IN piled high with paper.

The school's motto: *Animadverto Vestri. Remuneror Vestri. Vindico Vestri* was pinned to the wall behind him. It means: *See Yourself. Reward Yourself. Punish Yourself.*

There was a guest chair propped against the wall and in it was Mr Carter.

"Sit down, please," ordered Principal Hollerings.

"But Mr Carter—"

Mr Carter put out his palm and then pointed to the chair opposite Principal Hollerings. I opened my mouth, but then shut it again, plonking myself in the chair. I couldn't believe it — Mr Carter just gave me the hand!

"Please change your tone to one more suitable for the severity of this situation," said Principal Hollerings.

"Can't you just ring my mum?" I suggested.

"Miss Boans, please don't talk out of turn when you are addressing — actually, we have."

"Really? You mean you managed to make contact? That's

amazing! You must teach me how to do that."

"Miss Boans!" Principal Hollerings' thin lips grimaced.

Seriously, I had no idea what was wrong with me. I couldn't help it. When someone attacks me I have to fight back. Isn't that survival? Didn't my mum teach me that?

"I managed to get in contact with your mother after Mr Carter alerted me to your…sudden departure yesterday."

"Good."

"Indeed, Miss Boans. I would be more than happy to despatch you to your mother to let the two of you sort out your behaviour. If not for the fact that she told me she is flying out for two weeks as of this morning. Did she not discuss this with you when you so promptly arrived home yesterday?"

"No. I didn't see my mother when I got home yesterday. She must have come home at some point because I woke up to find — er, *lunch* — in the fridge. I don't know. I must have slept through her leaving."

Principal Hollerings shot a look at Mr Carter, who remained glassy-eyed.

"Your mother finds it fit to leave a seventeen-year-old—"

"Sixteen."

"*Sixteen*-year-old daughter at home by herself while she jets off for two weeks? Extraordinary!"

I shrugged. "My mother is a very busy woman. I'm pretty independent. I made spag-bog-for-one for dinner last night."

"Miss Boans," said Principal Hollerings. He folded

his fingers together into a tepee. "I alerted your mother to your circumstances yesterday and do you know what she told me?"

"What? I mean, what, *sir*?"

"She told me to deal with it myself. *As I see fit*. Barrister Boans may be a minor celebrity, but as the principal of this school, I expect more than that from her. *As I see fit*! Extraordinary."

Principal Hollerings was staring at me in such a way that I began to get angry about who was supposed to be in the wrong here. Did he really think it was me? Well maybe I thought it was him for humiliating me over my embarrassment of a mother. Maybe I thought it was my mother herself, with her Gucci handbag hanging deceptively on the coat rack, but the rest of her somewhere else.

"Miss Boans, we much prefer the input of parents when it comes to matters like this, but seeing as this is not possible, then we must discipline you here."

"Fine," I said.

Which brought me back to the school motto, hanging behind Principal Hollerings' balding head. *See Yourself. Reward Yourself. Punish Yourself.*

Somewhere along the line, some old men like Principal Hollerings, who didn't have any children themselves, decided they were going to base the school rules on something a dead Greek philosopher, like Hippocraps or whatever, once said about democracy.

The parents couldn't get enough of it, all trying to move to East Rivermoor and clamouring to shove fistfuls of school fees down Principal Hollerings' pants. It was going to be all about the students being treated as individuals, all their needs and special personalities taken care of. Obviously all the things our parents thought they deserved once.

In reality, it meant we could pretty much do what we wanted, as long as that didn't mean getting into trouble. Then it became a little complicated, since we were supposed to act like adults and adults weren't supposed to do things like skip classes. And just 'cos Hollerings couldn't rap us across the knuckles, it didn't mean we got anything less painful.

See Yourself. Reward Yourself. Punish Yourself.

"Is there anything you want to say for yourself?"

Anyone would think this was my last rites. "Can I please talk about what happened yesterday? I think there has been some mistake—"

Principal Hollerings sighed. "We can talk about yesterday until we are quite blue in the face, Miss Boans. The fact is that you marched out of a classroom — with a new student in tow no less — then disappeared. The fact is that you committed an offence. And what would have happened if you had become involved in an accident when you left the school grounds?'

Yeah, as if he would care if I got run over. He'd only care about being hauled to court by my mum, and the Parent and School Committee running after him carrying pitchforks and burning torches.

"As you are well aware, since we are a progressive school, we ask all our students to participate in setting their own punishment agendas. You are a good student, Miss Boans. Very consistent in your marks and your history teacher is very complimentary of your character, so that will all be held in your favour."

I stared at Mr Carter. Mr Carter still refused to meet my eyes.

"Can I do detention with Mr Carter then?" I put on a stricken face.

The corners of Principal Hollerings' mouth pulled up into a smile. Principal Hollerings never smiled. When he did it usually signalled something cruel and unusual. Something like *big* trouble.

"Do you honestly believe that will be punishment enough?"

"Yes," I replied. "After all, didn't I run away from History? I must hate it."

"Let's see about that," replied Principal Hollerings. "I have asked another student to help judge on this matter. Bring her in Mr Carter, please."

I twisted around in the uncomfortable Eames wire chair, currently etching a criss-cross brand into my flesh, to see a familiar blonde being ushered into the room. Jane Ayres gave me a sickening smile.

"Miss Ayres."

"Principal Hollerings."

Jane sat down next to Mr Carter. She crossed her leg and made sure the tip of her foot almost touched Mr Carter's leg. I hated her.

"Miss Ayres, I have asked you in this morning to help assist with this matter. Thank you for inconveniencing yourself."

"No inconvenience at all," replied Jane.

"You are in Miss Boans' History class, I believe?"

Jane inclined her head slightly by way of a nod. I wanted to knock her head off.

"Miss Boans here thinks that detention with Mr Carter will be sufficient for the incident yesterday. As a witness, and because we like our students to adjudicate on behalf of each other as equals, what would be your opinion?"

"What?" I exclaimed loudly as Jane opened her mouth to speak. "She was bloody outside the entire time! She didn't see or hear a single—"

"Miss Boans!" Principal Hollerings raised his croaky voice. "Do not speak out of line again, do you hear?"

"As I understand," said Jane softly. "Miss Boans is a very *attentive* History student. In fact, if I am not mistaken, History is her favourite subject."

"Then," said Principal Hollerings, "why would she suddenly depart class?"

"I believe, personally," replied Jane, "that it has something to do with…interjectory factors. The influence of the new student she was with perhaps."

I didn't know what "interjectory" meant, but I sure knew what she was trying to imply.

"Noted," said Principal Hollerings. "In that case detention with Mr Carter will not be acceptable. And I will assign another student to be — what do you young ones call it — *buddies* with the new student, this Miss Dashwood. Thank you Miss Ayres."

If Jane could have beamed any harder right then, her entire head would have exploded. She went to get out of her seat, but Principal Hollerings signalled for her to sit down again.

"Since you are so helpful Miss Ayres, what would you deem to be sufficient punishment for Miss Boans?"

Now hang on. I'm pretty sure this wasn't in our School Charter.

"I don't wish to pass judgement or participate in hearsay…"

"Go on," said Principal Hollerings.

"I believe Miss Boans holds a personal dislike of the canteen. She believes the food is lacking for her tastes. Perhaps her efforts can be directed to helping…improve the service?"

Principal Hollerings turned to me. "Indeed Miss Boans, is that true?"

"The canteen is a complete load of—"

"Then it is decided. Miss Boans, you will give up your lunch breaks and serve one week as canteen assistant."

"But—!"

"Is there anything further Miss Ayres?"

"I think Miss Boans should be transferred to another History class."

"Done!"

If Principal Hollerings had a little wooden hammer, he would be smacking it down and shouting "Sold! One Miss Eliza Boans to the nasty plastic blonde on the right!"

Principal Hollerings folded his arms happily. "You are all dismissed now."

"Mr Carter—"

But Mr Carter turned away from me.

I stared from Principal Hollerings, looking pleased with himself behind his desk, to Mr Carter with his cold shoulder toward me and Jane Ayres with the smile on her face that said all her Christmases had come at once. I turned and stormed out of the office.

I almost knocked Neil over. Well, more like I almost knocked myself out on him.

Every time I thought of Neil, in my head he's always five years old and, inexplicably, *blond*. And not so *tall*. Things have obviously changed. I took off without a word.

"Wait for me!" shouted Lexi as I hurried past. "Seeya, Neil."

"Seeya Alex…and Eliza," he added softly.

Lexi caught me by the elbow. "What was all that about?"

"Crap! I've been kicked out of Carter's class."

"So what does this have to do with Jane Ayre-head?"

"Absolutely nothing. And yet they let her decide everything! I can't believe it."

"You did break the rules and skip school, though," said Lexi. "I guess you can't argue against that."

"Yeah, I know," I sighed.

"So you'll have to switch to Mr Gubler's class? Apparently he's so boring that he even bores himself to sleep. They can't afford to jeopardise your marks. You need to get your mum onto this."

"My mother's gone interstate for two weeks and didn't think to tell me. I had to find out through Principal Hollerings. You reckon she will care what teacher I do or don't have for History?"

Lexi became quiet.

"And even worse, I have canteen duty. For a week!"

"I'm sorry," said Lexi and she put her arm over my shoulder.

"Maybe you'll get to do your detention with Neil. I tell you what, he's got some major unresolved issues. Remind me again why we're still friends with him?"

"I don't know."

"Neil is your friend, really. Not ours. Maybe you should drop him."

"Maybe," I said.

I don't know. He's been our friend — *my friend* — forever. Maybe it's because our parents knew each other before we did; maybe 'cos we were born three days apart. Maybe it's because we're both Sagittarians. Maybe it's in the stars. It could be one of many things. Neil is just...Neil. Even if he's a little tapped in the head.

"First class is English Lit. Yay. Come on, let's go," said Lexi and she pulled me into a right turn.

◆❖

"Alexandria — *Lexi* — sounds like a very close friend," says Dr Fadden, stating the obvious. He pauses for confirmation.

"Lexi is my best friend," I reply and I rub my eyes hard with balled-up fists. "I know she is still here. I just know it. Can I please talk to her, or at least pass a message to her?"

"No," replies Dr Fadden. "Not after what happened in the kitchen before. You will have to work with me, just like you are doing right now, to regain my trust. Then maybe you might get something in return."

I can't believe Dr Fadden is spinning this around. Maybe he thinks he can use his reverse psychology thing on me.

"But Lexi has nothing to do with this. She doesn't deserve this! You have to believe me."

"Alexandria was found with blood spattered all over her clothes. That is a fact," says Dr Fadden. "You will have to provide me with more than just your pleas to get her out of here. Now, would you like me to go and make you another cup of coffee if it will make you more comfortable?"

I am shivering now, despite this stuffy room. When I put the tasteless mug of coffee to my lips, the remnants are stone cold. My clothes are covered with dried tears, dust and blood. No one can tell me now that they can give me anything that would make me one bit more comfortable.

"Yes," I say through my numbness and then I add, "please."

Dr Fadden nods and gets up to leave the room. He locks the door behind him.

three

Sixteen. There's nothing *sweet* about sixteen. Especially when practically everyone else is born at the beginning of the year and is already seventeen. Already able to drive. Already gone. And here I still am with my feet in the same place. I am so scared of being left behind. My mother says that's what puts the aggressive streak in me.

"Thank you," I say to Dr Fadden.

I wipe my nose on the back of my hand and take another sip of coffee. It tastes just like the one before: horrible.

"How did your punishment at the canteen go?"

"Bad."

"In what way?"

"Well if you think the food there *looks* disgusting, you should see how they actually *make* it."

There I am again, trying to be brave. On the inside I shake like the canteen jelly.

"Is that all?"

"What do you mean *is that all?* Have you even seen the beef goulash?"

"Serious, Eliza."

"Right. You want to know if I suffered a traumatic episode that would later become my psychological trigger?

"Something like that."

I realise I'm twisting a piece of hair so tightly around my knuckle that my finger has turned purple. I put my hand back into my lap.

"No." I reply.

I stare at him. I try and stare at him with all my hate so that I can burn a hole in his face.

"Hmm." He scribbles something down.

The doctor's been writing notes ever since we met. His notebook is bound in brown leather, just like Dr Fadden himself. Wrapped in his taupe-coloured shirt and brown leather jacket. His trousers are those cream slacks middle-aged men wear once they, like, grow out of normal pants. I wonder if that moment is a conscious and horrifying one.

"You know Eliza, I think you're lying to me again. Deep on the inside, I know you have a lot to say."

We lock eyes with each other. I plan to win the contest, but we're interrupted by a hard knock on the door. It opens without permission and the Chief Inspector sticks his head through. I don't know his name. The other cops call him *sir*. All I know is that he makes me sick to my stomach when I look at him. He's got hair that looks like it's been slicked back with chip oil and a moustache like a porn star.

"Fadden — the girl's mother is outside with her lawyer."

"Did you hear that?" whispers Dr Fadden, leaning towards me. "Your mother is here. Again."

"Brian, we cannot refuse them counsel. I will have to let the lawyer in."

"No!" I say loudly.

The room goes quiet. They both turn to look at me.

"There is no *we. I* am refusing counsel. I don't want to talk to any lawyer. I only want to talk to Dr Fadden."

The chief stares at me with his eyelids peeled right back. It's a scary sight. One eye stares right at me while the other stares at the doctor.

"Brian, I need to talk to you. Now!"

Dr Fadden looks at me, shrugs and gets up. The heated words begin even before the door clicks shut. Meh. I'm used to shouting; my parents used to fight like that all the time.

My eyes instantly zoom to the notebook and manila folder. I sweep my eyes around the white room. This could be another trick. Maybe there's a two-way mirror and they're watching me right now…but this room is solid brick and I don't think the government has enough money for mirror-that-looks-like-ugly-seventies-brick-wall-spy-technology. Maybe he just trusts me.

Sucker.

I lean over the desk and grab the notebook. I wonder who gave it to him. It looks expensive, and it smells earthy, like the Tom Ford cologne my father used to wear. I quickly draw back when I realise I'm pressing my nose against the cover. Three female faces stare at me with empty eyes and snakes for hair. What the hell? I almost drop the notebook in horror.

I try to flip it open, but I realise my wrist doesn't work.

Wow. I sigh and drop the notebook back down on the table. I can't do it. I don't want to know what he has written about me. What he thinks about me. Right now even *I* don't want to think about myself. Later I'll just say I felt bad about invading his privacy.

No one said anything about the manila folder though. It is just some ordinary, beat-up bit of cream card. Nothing that says *don't go there.*

I take out the photo of Lexi from before. Behind it is a photo of Ella.

She looks shocking. I perk up. Maybe I can make copies and plaster it all over school with a speech bubble. *Hi, I'm Ella and I finally got arrested by the fashion police for looking this bad.* That would serve her right.

But what am I thinking? School is over. Come next year everyone will be going to uni. Many will go to prestigious colleges in the UK and the States and be living away from home for the first time.

Where will I be?

There's a photo of me too. So this is how I look as a criminal. Like an arrested hooker. There's more mascara than face. When they made me line up against the wall for a photo I wanted to stand there and pull faces, but I ended up standing very still holding the placard because I was so scared. The strands of hair that fall across my face look like bleeding cuts.

Then there is Marianne. To my surprise Marianne doesn't look too bad in her mug shot. She has flaky lips and her hair is limp, but she looks calm. Almost angelic. Almost innocent.

Even though the words that still echo in my head are the ones *I am sick of him, just finish the bastard off.*

A deep breath wells inside me. Without Marianne, I find myself weak all of a sudden. I miss her. I spent so much time trying to put her down that I never stopped to think how lonely I would be when I finally found myself alone.

My stomach makes the hugest growl. I'm starving. I realise I can't remember the last time I ate.

"Anorexics make it seem so easy, but it's actually a bitch trying to stay slim," said Lexi, scoffing down a white bread sandwich, even though today was Wednesday and her non-lunch day.

It was sunny and I was in a good mood. We'd decided to sit on the grass by the lake. There were swallows everywhere. Black crescents in the sky, skimming the grass almost on their bellies. Lexi says the swallows are shaped like blades and are bad luck. I don't blame the swallows.

"I am so sorry for your suffering," said Marianne, eyeing Lexi as she pushed a stray piece of cheese into her mouth. Lexi shot her a dirty look and continued eating.

"I bet Jane Ayres is anorexic," I said. "I have never seen her eat anything except salad. No, hang on…I saw Jane Ayres eat a *Maccas* salad once. She must have been off her diet that day."

"But just look at her," said Lexi. "I would kill to be that skinny. Do you know what I hate? People who go, 'oh, you're so lucky to be so slim'. On the inside I'm thinking, 'honey, luck has nothing to do with it. Do you know how much I have to starve and exercise to make it look this easy?'"

"Precisely," replied Marianne. "Just the two things you are doing right now, starving yourself on that sandwich and exercising flat on your bum."

"Oh, shut up why don't you?" was all Lexi could counter with, and she pouted. Marianne looked proud of herself.

I stared at Marianne and her perfectly flat stomach.

"You're so mean," I said. "You're like one of those people who upload pictures of themselves where they look really hot and the other person looks like shit."

"Thanks," replied Marianne.

"Hey look, there's Ella!" I stuck my arm up and waved, glad to change the topic. Ella made a u-turn in our direction. Beside me, Lexi and Marianne exchanged looks.

"Hey Ella, how's it going with your new — what does Hollerings call it? — *buddies*? Are you even allowed to say hello to me?"

"Thank you so much for asking," replied Ella. "I can't even begin to tell you — I'm having the craziest time! So many faces to put names to and this school is just enormous! I can't believe the size of the wings, I mean the bathrooms here are probably the size of classrooms in other schools — but anyway, it's okay, I can talk to you."

Huh. I guess that's Ella-speak for *yes*.

"Come sit down," I said and patted the grass beside me.

Ella smiled and plonked herself down. From her satchel she drew out a brown paper lunchbag with a square, sandwich-shaped lump in the middle.

"Not buying your lunch today?" Marianne quipped.

I flashed a look at Marianne. She looked back at me with a straight, innocent face.

"I — I had a think about the canteen lunch and I decided Eliza's right. It doesn't taste very nice. So I got my mum to make me a sandwich instead. Ham and cheese."

"Oh really?" said Marianne, wrinkling her nose. "I don't eat ham. Meat is so mean. Personally, I find the entire farming industry quite barbaric."

Luckily no one was listening to Marianne.

"Hey, nice bracelet," said Ella looking down at Lexi's hand.

"Um, thanks," replied Lexi. She lifted her arm and shifted the beads around her wrist self-consciously. "I made it myself."

"Beautiful stones. Cat's Eyes aren't they?"

"That's right," replied Lexi.

"I make jewellery myself too. Have you seen that new craft supplies store that just opened near us? Down on the Strip, you know that has all the boutique stores? Maybe we can both go and check it out sometime."

"Sure," said Lexi. "Maybe we can." She took her wrist back from Ella. I watched a small smile spread across her lips.

"Lexi makes the nicest jewellery ever," said Marianne lazily. "I don't think anyone could possibly make anything as nice as our Lexi."

"Oh believe me, I make pretty nice jewellery," chirped Ella.

Now, Ella was either feeling really brave or really foolish and hadn't seen the souring look on Marianne's face. I'd put my bets on it being the latter.

"I'll bring in some samples of my work tomorrow to show

you. Or if you like, we can all go over to my place after school. My mum taught me everything I know. I actually come from a really long line of craft makers. My grandmother—"

"Fascinating," interrupted Marianne. "You know, honey, we would love to go over to your place, but I have piano lessons after school today and Lexi—"

"We'll go," said Lexi. "And Mari, I believe your piano lessons are actually on a Thursday."

"Great!" exclaimed Ella happily. "Mummy has been asking when I would bring some of my new friends over. She's so excited about meeting you all. She said it's so great for me to associate with some real Priory girls. Especially you, Eliza, we've read so much about your mum in the newspapers."

"Ah…yeah." I said, with an eye on Marianne whose tanned face was looking decidedly more red than golden.

"Tell us how you're getting along at Priory then," I asked quickly.

"Oh, fabulously," replied Ella. "In fact I went up to reception yesterday and the secretaries there were in a mess, papers everywhere because they're trying to computerise the old filing system. Since I have the best computer skills I offered to help."

"That's nice," said Lexi, the interest fading from her face.

"Well, I found this in the rubbish and I thought you might be interested in it, Eliza."

I looked at the dirty index card Ella held out eagerly. I skimmed the contents and my mouth dropped open.

Lexi decided she was interested again and snatched the card off me.

"No way!"

"It's true," said Ella. "Jane Ayres was actually born Jane Air. A-I-R. Appears she's changed the spelling and added the 's' to the end of it herself."

"Jane Air! That's excellent!" exclaimed Lexi. "Now we know what that nasty smell is that always lingers around her — the one that makes her turn up her own nose!"

"So!" added Ella eagerly, "We can say that without her fancy Ayres she is just — a plain Jane."

Lexi looked at me with a straight face, but she couldn't help it. She cracked up. Ella looked delighted. I started laughing as well and Ella took that as a cue that she could laugh too. We'd forgotten all about Marianne, who suddenly interrupted with—

"— If this is the type of mature talk we are going to waste our lunch time with, then I'm going to go and find more stimulating company elsewhere."

"But Marianne," I said to her, spluttering. "That is, like, the best thing ever!"

Marianne grabbed the index card from Lexi and chucked it onto the grass. A small gust of wind sent it rolling away down the hill toward the lake.

"And Eliza. Why are you here having lunch with us anyway? Aren't you supposed to be at the canteen doing detention?"

"Crap!" I said and stood up. "So I am."

Ella prepared to stand up too, but Lexi grabbed hold of her by the wrist. "Stay," she said gently. "Help me get the card back before it blows right under Hollerings' nose."

Marianne stormed off.

I threw one last look at the vision of Lexi and Ella chasing Jane Ayres' old identity in the wind. Then I turned back and ran after Marianne.

◆❖

A disembodied hand gently sweeps the photos in front of me to the side. It deposits a heavenly smelling paper bag, along with a tall white cardboard cylinder. I take the top off the cylinder. *Mmm. Cappuccino.* I grab at the plastic spoon greedily and start shovelling at the chocolate-dusted foam.

I look up to see Dr Fadden slowly walking to his side of the table. He looks grim. He seems surprised to see his brown notebook still sitting there. Undisturbed.

"Don't worry, I didn't look in it. Not that sort of girl."

He nods appreciatively, though I know he is searching my face. I think he could probably do with the affirmation.

"What are those *things* on the cover"

"Greek chthonic deities."

"Is that what they taught you in anthropology school?"

"I quite enjoyed the study of human behaviour as influenced by myth and superstition, yes."

"Is that how you ended up with a useless degree? Your

girlfriend nagged you about getting a real job, so now you're stuck doing this crap?"

See? I reckon I can read him like a book too.

"My mum would never let me choose a degree like that."

I meant for the words to come out cutting, but instead they make me sound weak and like I feel sorry for myself. I steer away from them.

"Where have you been?"

"For a walk," Dr Fadden replies.

Inside the brown paper bag is a raspberry muffin, still warm. It even has pictures of little raspberries printed on the paper case. Sorta sweet, if you like kitsch.

"I am told by my female colleague that this is the best muffin in town. I've heard that it's impossible just to eat one." He points to the dusted top. "So that might not be just innocent icing sugar."

At least he thinks the icing sugar is innocent, I think to myself. *Good for you, Doc.*

I take a bite of the muffin. Dr Fadden watches me.

"Your *friend* is right. This is a really good muffin."

Dr Fadden nods encouragingly.

"So who is she? Is she on this taskforce too? I could probably guess which one; there aren't too many females here. It's pretty testosterone-heavy."

"I ask the questions around here," cautions Dr Fadden.

I try to look at his face, but he keeps his head down. He gathers up the pile of photos and slaps one in front of me.

"Tell me about her."

It is Marianne. He stabs his finger on the photograph and gets her in the forehead.

In my mind I see the dusty ground, the hot sun, a girl's scream…the blade of the knife breaking through skin and into flesh…

"That's Marianne," I reply.

Dr Fadden looks annoyed. I give him a fake smile.

"Good luck to whichever loser you have trying to break her."

"What do you want Eliza?" The doctor suddenly appears to lose his cool. "For me to say congratulations? Or an apology from me for what you have done?"

Well Dr F, no one apologised when they took us and threw us into this hell-hole. My head hurts so much. Maybe I need an aspirin. Or ten.

"Eliza — Eliza eyes up here!"

"What now? My head hurts…"

"It's because you haven't eaten for twenty-four hours. Finish your muffin."

I take another bite. The smell of vanilla and berries is divine, but in my mouth, it feels like dirt and tastes like nothing.

"Do you know what I regret?"

I can hear Dr Fadden breathing.

"That we never listened to Marianne in the first place. Marianne never wanted Ella to join our group. If we had listened to her, then none of this would have happened."

Dr Fadden drops his shoulders; he looks almost disappointed. I know he's waiting for me to show regret. Then maybe he might start to feel sorry for me.

"I think after all this I never want to make new friends ever again."

"Good. Where you're probably headed you won't get a chance."

"Fine," I reply loudly. "Then I am glad that I tried to make it up to Marianne, and Lexi too, and put things right. So not only do I *not* regret it, I'm glad I did it."

Neil said to me once that in the times of desperation, you have to force yourself to make a decision.

It's your choice, he said. *Us or them. So choose.*

"Wait!" I shouted to Marianne as I ran to catch up with her.

"Don't you have to be somewhere?" Marianne muttered. "Mrs Wally is going to be so mad when you rock up at the canteen, oh, *twenty minutes late*, for your first detention."

"I know where I have to be," I replied. "Where are *you* going?"

"Why are you interested? Why don't you go back and play with Lexi and your new friend? I could tell you were having a good time. I'm just…going to Chem early."

"What?"

Marianne patted the pile of papers in her arms. She beamed like a proud parent.

"I've had a go at the exam papers from the past ten years. Professor McFarlane has agreed to do some extra marking for me."

"You're crazy, you know," I replied, trying to laugh it off.

Marianne stopped walking. "What is it now?"

"You know, to even take that class. I'm not surprised it only has two people in it. If this school weren't so rich, they would fire Nazi-tastic old McFarlane. I can't believe you and Neil are the only ones stupid enough to brave him."

Marianne arms tightened on her stack of neatly stapled papers.

"It's not his fault that the others couldn't hack it. At least Neil and I are smart. And at least we are choosing subjects based on the quality of the teachers and not—" Marianne shot me a veiled look, "—because of their popularity."

"I think Lexi likes Ella," I said, changing the subject.

"That's nice."

I stared at Marianne's side profile. I relished the fact that she couldn't actually look me in the face right now. Her long blonde hair was coiled into an intricate bun at the back of her head with wispy bits around her face. She looked like an impossibly beautiful Greek marble carving.

"Can you believe she had the guts to take Jane Ayres' record from the old biddies up in reception?"

Marianne shook her head. "When has stealing been a quality you look for in a friend?"

"Why can't you just give her a chance, Mari?" I sighed.

"Trust me, if I wasn't trying to give her a chance I would have banned her from hanging out with us from the very beginning."

My mouth dropped open. I curled it back into a smile.

"What did you say?"

Marianne said nothing.

"Hang *on*. It's not for you to say who this group associates with. You are *not*, Marianne, the leader of this group."

Marianne's hand shot up and touched her cheek. It glowed red like I had just slapped it. She pushed past me and hurried off again. This time I let her go.

"Say hi to Neil for me, won't you?" I called out to her.

It's harsh, but it's true. Marianne is not the leader. *I am*. I say who stays and who goes. I am the one who holds this group together. I will not let Marianne think that she is the boss of me. She just needs a good kick once in a while as a reminder.

The lunch-hall was packed and smelt like feet and rancid cheese. Mrs Wally greeted me inside the kitchen with crossed arms and a face like the centre of Hell.

"Get out there and start working missy, you are twenty-five minutes late. And lunch is only forty minutes long."

"Sorry. I forgot," I replied, tying the disgusting, smelly apron around me.

"Don't think that I'll forget. I am noting this down for the fury

Principal. He will, I'm sure, see that you make this time up."

Mrs Wally flashed a particularly nasty grin with her 400-watt chemically whitened teeth.

"Looks like you will be stuck with me well into next week, huh?"

I made a face, but I didn't answer back. As much as I was tempted to say something smart, I valued not having to work here *forever* a lot more. I winced as Mrs Wally took the gum out of her mouth and stuck it under the kitchen counter.

"Excuse me. Are you sure this is chicken?"

I spun around to find Neil pointing to one of the steaming trays in the bainmarie. Thank God, I thought I'd never get away from that hag. I smiled and walked up to him. Neil smiled back. He had big brown eyes like Bambi. So there we were. Separated by steaming glass.

"I guess so, if that's what the label says…"

I looked at the four dishes. They looked identical. I shrugged.

Neil gave it the benefit of doubt and ladled some onto his plate. It landed with a sickening plop.

"I've never seen you eat canteen food."

"Neither have I," replied Neil.

He leaned closer to the glass. I found myself doing the same thing.

"You see, I was going to make myself a sandwich this morning, but then I found we had no ham left. So I thought I would make a cheese sandwich. Except there was no cheese either. I couldn't even make a margarine sandwich 'cos the margarine tub was empty. Then I found we had no bread so I gave up."

"Oh."

"My dad said he was doing the groceries yesterday. And he must have because I found two bottles of Scotch in the pantry. I guess he must have forgotten to, like, buy food."

"How is your dad?"

"Drunk, I think," replied Neil.

I tried to change the subject.

"Nice tie. Very retro," I said.

"Thanks."

East Rivermoor is a vanity wonderland. Designer shoes, expensive haircuts, makeup, skin-tight clothes — and that's just the boys.

The girls are expected to wear a white dress shirt with a grey skirt and the boys grey trousers and a tie. But we can pimp our outfits any which way we like. I'd gotten my mother's tailor to shorten all my skirts because I have to admit it, I have a nice pair of legs. Lexi has white Chinese frog buttons sewn on her shirt cuffs, and Marianne slit her sleeves right up to the elbow and put rows of tiny silver buttons all along them. Behind Neil, a whole spectrum of different ties moved through the lunch-hall like a testosterone rainbow. Hollerings doesn't care as long as you show some pretence of trying to fit in. They want us to all be the same, but individual. Independent, but controlled. It's all very PC.

"Hey, you never told me what detention you ended up with."

"I have to stay behind for a week and clean the cleaners' cupboard," replied Neil drolly. "Fitting, I suppose."

"You are not here to chat up boys!" Mrs Wally's sharp voice cut through the sound of sizzling oil from the kitchen. That cranky old cow was watching me like a hawk.

"That's ten bucks, thanks."

Neil passed me a crinkled note between his index and middle fingers.

"Enjoy your lunch."

Neil shrugged and picked up his tray. My hand grew a mind of its own and went to touch my blazer pocket, where the postcard still was. I forced it back down.

"Well, well, well," said the voice to my right that I knew only too well. It was the whiney voice of Jeremy Biggins.

"What do you want Biggins?"

"*Oooo*. Fiery, just like the hair. Is this the usual level of service?"

"No. This is the level of service I reserve especially for you, short-ass."

Jeremy Biggins' hair and face are usually the same colour: red. Right now though, that face was heading towards beetroot.

"Get me what I want nicely or I may ask to speak to your supervisor, Boans," he scowled. "Take-away black tea, thanks. One sugar."

In hindsight, it was a pretty lucky thing I made it a little cold. I smacked the cardboard cup down on the counter. Biggins paid for it with change. I threw the coins into the cash register and slammed it shut. Biggins took the lid off the cup. Then he threw the tea onto me.

"You little sh— *oww!*" I screamed.

The tea hit me right in the middle of my stomach and burned through the apron and onto the thin fabric of my shirt. I was lucky I had my trusty pair of thick high-waisted spanx underneath. I threw the apron off and grabbed a dirty cloth from the bench, dabbing furiously at my shirt.

"What the Heavens is happening out here!" echoed Mrs Wally as she approached from the kitchen. "Miss Eliza!"

"Crap!" I screamed again, jumping up and down. "I'm going to kill that— "

"Miss Eliza!" bellowed Mrs Wally. "You silly, clumsy girl!"

Silly? Clumsy? What the...?

It took me a while to comprehend that Mrs Wally thought I had done this to myself.

"No! Him!" I pointed toward Biggins, who at that moment was scurrying away through the crowd.

I turned to face Mrs Wally.

"Someone's gotta stop him!"

Someone apparently did. We heard a huge crash. Mrs Wally and I both stared at each other. Then we bolted for the side door. I made it out first; I had the smaller ass.

I pushed past a large mob of students. In the middle stood Jeremy Biggins, a smashed plate on the ground next to him. There was chicken cacciatore dripping down his head. In front of him stood Neil, with his empty tray still in his hands.

"That is it!" Mrs Wally exclaimed and grabbed my wrist. She clamped the other hand onto Neil's shoulder. I heard her mutter the word "children" under her breath, along with a few choice expletives.

"I will not have this. I am taking you both to the Principal's office right now!"

Neil was still holding onto his plastic tray as Mrs Wally pulled us toward the lunch-hall entrance. He passed it to a random tenth-grader in the crowd who hooted loudly and held the tray up in the air like a trophy.

Principal Hollerings was not in his office. We had to wait ten minutes, me with a huge cooling tea stain in the middle of my shirt, and Neil next to me, looking like he'd just murdered a chicken cacciatore. Mrs Wally paced back and forth smoking a cigarette.

"Excuse me, ma'am, but there's no smoking on school premises," I said. "You might give us children cancer."

"Butt out," replied Mrs Wally.

Apt choice of words, but I kept quiet. I didn't want to, like, blow Mrs Wally's mind with the irony.

I looked sideways at Neil.

Neil looked back and raised a sauce-speckled eyebrow at me. Guess he didn't know why it was us either. *Again*.

Principal Hollerings hurried up the hallway on his ebony cane with the gold eagle's head, the one that looks like a pimp's walking stick. He looked decidedly unimpressed when he saw the both of us sitting on the bench outside his office.

"Miss Boans, Mr Fernandes. What is this? I only saw the two of you on Tuesday? Which, incidentally, was yesterday."

"Principal Hollerings," said Mrs Wally. "These two students were responsible for the shenanigans out there. I caught Miss Eliza red-handed and this student—"

Mrs Wally pointed a false fingernail at Neil.

"—must be somehow involved because I saw him having a long and meaningful chat with the girl only two minutes earlier!"

"Miss Boans, explain yourself please," sighed the Principal.

"Jeremy Biggins threw a cup of tea at me."

"Pardon me?"

"Threw a cup of tea on me. As in he bought a cup of tea from me—"

"You mean to say that the young gentleman purchased a cup of tea off you with his own money, only to throw it back at you?"

"Yes. That's right. And for your own information I wouldn't call him a *gentleman*."

"Keep your personal observations to yourself please, Miss

Boans. Mrs Wally did you witness any of this?"

"No," replied Mrs Wally flatly and her face dropped as best as the botox would let it.

"But, sir!" I said, a little louder now. "Just because you have a grudge against me doesn't mean you can just refuse to believe me! I'm telling you the truth."

Principal Hollerings put a hand to his forehead. There was a horrible throbbing vein there.

"I ran into Mr Biggins on my way here. He said that Mr Fernandes slid the entire contents of his lunch onto his head. What do you have to say about that?"

Principal Hollerings stared expectantly at Neil. Mrs Wally turned to stare at Neil. I looked at Neil as well.

"It was an accident," replied Neil. "Jeremy was running. I thought that one of the school rules prohibits students from running indoors? He wasn't watching where he was going and he ran into, well — my lunch."

"Is this true?" exclaimed Principal Hollerings. "Did you see any of this occur, Mrs Wally?"

"No, unfortunately." Mrs Wally replied. You should have heard the disappointment in her voice.

"Miss Marianne Jones — the school's *best* student — and Miss Alexandria Gutenberg were both present, sir. I am sure they will serve as credible witnesses," added Neil.

Mrs Wally flashed him a suspicious look, but didn't say anything.

"Miss Jones and Miss Gutenberg?" Principal Hollerings

paused. "In that case, Mr Fernandes — consider this a warning. You are currently on detention, so I advise you be more vigilant with your behaviour. Miss Boans, I advise you to do the same. I am disappointed in the both of you. This is your last and most important term of study. Please do not neglect the reputation of Priory Grammar for the sake of your immature games. You are both dismissed."

Mrs Wally watched with a dumbstruck look on her face as Principal Hollerings waddled into his office.

"You're coming back to the canteen with me, missy," said Mrs Wally with her hand extended toward me.

The school bell sounded.

At Priory, they say that the sound of the traditional bell is too violent, so have replaced it with the soothing tones of the chimes that you hear in airports. It makes me think of all these students pacing back and forth through the wide glass halls with our heavy bags. Forever trying to get somewhere else.

"See you tomorrow then, Mrs Wally," I said to her and smiled. "I gotta get going to class now."

I pulled my school shirt free of my skirt and looked at the stain. Yuck. I started unbuttoning from the bottom and then stopped when I realised Neil was staring at me.

"Come on, I'll walk you to History. It's on the way to the Chemlab," he said.

We left quickly.

"Well, at least you know you're definitely at Priory. School of Hard Knocks, Jocks and Designer Frocks. We're not in

Hogwarts anymore, Hermione."

"You lied to Principal Hollerings," I said, looking at the ground. "About Lexi and Marianne being there. I can't believe it. Why would you do that?"

Neil smiled.

"You don't have to protect me, you know!"

"Of course I have to."

"I am not a weak little girl."

"Of course you are. The truth would crush you like the tiny flower you are."

I punched him in the arm. Then I realised that I was not five years old anymore and I stuck my hand behind my back.

"I'm sorry you wasted your lunch," I said.

"No problem. I accidentally tasted some when it splattered off Biggins. It was pretty horrible."

My mouth couldn't help but twitch upwards. I snuck a look at him. Sometimes I think Neil is cute. With his super-skinny frame, retro clothes and longish black hair that hangs in his eyes. But then I think of Neil when I knew him as a five-year-old, running around outside in his pyjamas with spaceships on them…

"Don't forget to tell your friends," said Neil.

"Tell them what?"

"About what they just saw. In case we are ever brought in for questioning. Seeya."

"Oh," I replied.

Neil winked and he was gone.

◆❖

In case we are ever brought in for questioning.

Isn't it funny? The things that we say, that come back to bite us. Maybe there's no such thing as innocent words after all.

four

It is evening now. The clock behind my head is pointing to eight o'clock. But what would I know? This room has no windows and the fluorescent light is on all the time, so for all I know it could be eight in the morning of the following day. Why should I care anyway?

I try not to think of Mum, but my thoughts wander to what she would say right now if it had been just another school night. On a day when she would actually decide to come home from work. It would be something like, *we should try that new Japanese up the road* or *have you seen Fluers du Mal's new summer menu? I simply lurve the sound of the duck leg confit. Yum.*

"Are you going home?" I ask Dr Fadden. "Don't you have a girlfriend or a family to go to?"

Dr Fadden looks at me with his unreadable brown eyes.

"No."

No to the going home part, or *no* to the girlfriend and family, I wonder.

"If you can help me wrap up this interrogation quickly then *you* might be able to go home."

"Why are you still stuck on that?" I ask. "It'll mean going home to my mother and I'd rather not see her again, *ever*. Write that down in your little notepad. So you don't forget."

"If that's all I'm going to get out of you then I might as well call it a day."

I look up at him.

"No, don't leave me!"

The doctor looks at his watch.

"Well, I've got to allow myself the luxury of, say, some semblance of ordinary life. I'm not the prisoner here after all. *You are.* I'm not going to suffer just because you want to."

"I am not a prisoner. I haven't been found guilty of anything." I grimace. "Wait, don't put me back in that horrible holding room. I think I saw a cockroach in there and …I don't want to be left alone."

Dr Fadden takes a good long look at me. I put on my most pitiful looking face. It's a good thing I'd been practising in front of my laptop recently, looking for something suitably *smexy* to update my avatar.

"Then tell me about the second body," says Dr Fadden casually.

I swallow. It feels like I am swallowing ball bearings. They go clunk when they hit the bowling ball sitting in my stomach.

"I don't want to talk about the first body; what makes you think I want to talk about the second one?"

"Because I know it's different."

"I — *we* — had nothing to do with that. Like I told you, I didn't even know about it until I was brought here."

I force myself to shut my mouth. That wasn't true, and I knew it.

"Come on, Eliza. I know and you know there's a connection. Give me a carrot here." Dr Fadden is pushing me like a goddamn pimp.

"I'll talk about Ella if you let me come with you. It was all her fault."

"Ella's been cleared and sent home. By the way, she spins a very different story."

"Take it or leave it."

Dr Fadden bites his bottom lip. His eyes search mine.

"Fine. But I'll get into trouble if they find out about this, so I'm warning you—"

"I won't try anything. Anyway, if you manage to get all the info out of me, doesn't 'the end justify the means' and all that Maccabelly or whatever crap?"

"Let's go," says Dr Fadden flatly.

"I've got blood spatter," I say and I pinch at my school shirt.

Dr Fadden's solution is to give me a woman's blue trench coat. It's not glamorous and it smells a little like cat piss, but it fits. I wonder if it's an ex-evidence sample and I'm rubbing myself in someone's guilty DNA.

Dr Fadden grabs me by the arm. "Let's go now."

This seems to be another recurring motif. The me-being-dragged-around thing. Maybe I should just get used to it.

◆❖

On Monday we noticed something different about Ella. Something — or more precisely, someone — had altered her school blouse. The sleeves had been embroidered with a white silk pattern that crept gradually up the sides of her arms, and the shoulders had been pleated. I guess it's nice if you go for that whole Victorian picnic-at-hanging-rock-chic. Okay, I'll admit it. It looked stunning.

"Do you think Ella knows how to sew?" I said to Marianne as we strolled arm in arm toward the library. "That could really come in useful."

It is a pain getting to the library. It was designed by some snotty famous architect who agreed to build it on the condition it was on the other side of the lake. So it wouldn't be, like, touched or God forbid, actually used by the students. I mean, it's a *work of art*.

"Well, she knows how to do everything else doesn't she?" replied Marianne bitterly. "I went to look at dresses in Old Mooreland with my mother on the weekend and I couldn't find a single one I liked. I mean, I couldn't find anything that didn't have a gaping hole in the front, down the back, up the sides or a combination of all three."

I grinned. "I can't believe you've started looking already for the end-of-school ball. Oh, I forget — you're the head of the Ball Committee. So naturally, you have to look better than everyone else."

Marianne blushed and said nothing.

We enter the round, glass and metal library. If the library really was supposed to be a work of art, it would be less the National Gallery and more like the new limited edition giant cotton spool from Swarovski. Study desks like long metal operating tables gleam inside. In summer the library is burning hot and in winter it is freezing cold. Obviously this famous East Rivermoor architect didn't really think functionality was a big factor.

"I can't even believe you're on the Ball Committee! I have no idea how you're going to be able to suffer all those bimbos and supermodel wannabes.

"Have you ever heard of extra-curricular activities, Lizzie?" Marianne replied, grabbing the books out of her bag.

"My mother says it makes you a more accomplished person. Maybe you should try it some time."

"Yeah, yeah," I shot back. "The real question is — when are you going to do something for yourself for once and not your mother? I'll ask Ella who made the alterations for her."

"Thanks," said Marianne grudgingly. It meant that we had made up from the other day. It was her way of saying *that's okay* and my way of saying *I'm sorry*.

◆❖

"Why thank you!" beamed Ella. "It is really pretty and feminine, isn't it? I have no idea why anyone would wear the white dress shirt as it is."

If I was not mistaken, Ella was quite happy to wear that white dress shirt *as it was* just last week, but I didn't say anything.

"Did you, um, do it yourself?"

"Oh, no. I mean, I can cross stitch, long stitch and lacework, you name it —but I can't take credit for this. My mum did it on the weekend. She's a much more accomplished needlewoman than I."

"Did it take her long?"

"Not at all. My mum makes all her own clothes because she doesn't like, er, modern clothing. She's trying to 'bring Regency back'. Have you heard of Dot & Dash Designs? Well, that's my mum. Why do you ask?"

Have I heard of *Dot & Dash* Designs? *Hello* — does Jane

Ayres thinks the sun shines out of her own ass? If there's a couture label that Eliza Boans has not heard of, then it's one that doesn't exist. Dot & Dash happen to be this year's *numero uno up-and-coming talent to watch* as decreed by the *East Rivermoor Eye*. I thought it was named after two separate designers. Now I realised that the name refers to one. Mrs Dorothy Dashwood.

I replied with something that contained more drool than legitimate English. I composed myself and said coolly, "Well, actually Marianne asks. It's to do with, um, the end-of-school-ball and she needs a dress that is kind of...*special*."

"Oh, of course. Are you all still coming over to meet my mum? She has a whole sewing room with the most delicious gowns. She sells them to really exclusive clients who pay a lot for them, that's how we could afford to move to East Rivermoor..." Ella trailed off. "But, of course, she won't charge Marianne. Will you come over today? It will be so much fun!"

I thought about my Principal Hollerings-issued restraining order. And I thought, stuff it. I should be able to see Ella out of school hours if I want to. And after all, she was the one inviting me.

"Of course," I replied. "The other two will be super excited when I tell them."

Would they ever. To have the opportunity to go to the home of the creator of Dot & Dash? They would literally *kill* for the opportunity.

"Meet you at the gates after school then. I have to rush to Human Bio now. Oh, and sorry I can't look for you during lunch, I've promised to be somewhere else. Bye!"

I watched as Ella hitched her schoolbag onto her shoulder and waved excitedly at someone in the crowd of migrating students.

That someone was Jane Ayres. I watched the two of them walk together head-to-head until they become swallowed up by the white and grey undertow. So I guess that's who her new *buddy* is. I made up my mind to keep that piece of info away from Marianne. I knew it would only make her cranky.

"So, you're interested in fashion then?"

Dr Fadden has left his notebook behind at the station and is trying to make small talk.

"What girl isn't?" I sniff and wipe my nose.

It is disgustingly humid outside, but it is the most exhilarating experience of my life. After being locked up in a little white box, the blackening sky outside is beautiful. The lights of the cafés and shops make my eyes water. I pull the stranger's trench coat closer to my body. I feel so small, so pathetic. Like the evening sky could reach down and crush me there and then, without anyone even noticing — or caring.

"We won't go too far away, is that okay with you?"

I nod furiously.

I wonder why he asks my opinion. Is it human nature

I wonder, this unconscious need to please? To be affirmed?

"This place does decent food and coffee. It's got air-conditioning anyway."

Dr Fadden opens the door for me and I hop inside, rocking on my heels, fists balled up inside the trench coat pockets.

"You come here for dinner every night?"

Dr Fadden does something with his head that could mean either yes or no.

"Burger and chips?" he asks.

"Okay. Can you make sure it is a lean meat burger? And no ketchup please. I don't do ketchup."

I sit down at a table for two that is covered in a chequered plastic tablecloth that is sticky to the touch. Dr Fadden orders at the counter. I look down at my feet; I forgot I'm still wearing my new Manolo Blahniks. I kick the straps off impatiently. The backs of my feet are all bruised and my toes ache.

"My mum's in the legal system too," I tell Dr Fadden as he sits down opposite me. "She's always schmoozing it up in cocktail lounges, so shouldn't you be somewhere nicer?"

I see his eyes flutter toward the ceiling for a micro second.

"You hate being here." I narrow my eyes at him. "When you were young and still had dreams did you ever think it'd end up like this?"

"I like my job," says the doctor. Well good on him. At least I know he likes one thing.

"We are not here on a play-date to talk about me. You know we only need to talk about one person. Here, I ordered a drink for you."

An angry-looking waitress plonks a tall metal cup in front of me. Guess I don't blame her. If I worked here I would be angry too.

Maybe for the first time in my life I can relate to someone else; maybe working at the canteen has changed me. Just imagine what my father would say if he hadn't been absent for ten years already. He would say, "Eliza, you are learning to be humble, I'm proud of you."

I look inside the metal cup. It is a strawberry milkshake. I pick out the sinking plastic straw.

"This is a straight straw. Can I get a bendy one?"

Dr Fadden motions for the waitress without flinching. The same waitress comes over and she looks at me with contempt. She goes away and comes back with a red and white striped straw. A bendy one.

"By the way, this is skim milk isn't it?" I dip the straw in and take a sip.

Oops. About the "humble" thing. I guess I'll have to try again.

"Can you get me a drink as well?" The doctor asks.

"What would you like?"

"I don't care. As long as it's served up in a wine glass."

The waitress gives an understanding nod and one last glare at me before she walks off.

"I'm not his precocious Gen-Y daughter y'know," I mumble more to myself than anyone else. "I'm not that bad."

"You know according to phrenology, women are seen as incapable of committing crimes because they are considered the weak and passive sex," says the doctor.

"Excuse me?"

"Facial profiling. It says that women who are born criminals will exhibit physical characteristics such as excessive body hair, wrinkles and an abnormal cranium."

My hand flies to my face to touch the space between my eyebrows and I can see something resembling a smile on his face.

"That's not true!" I frown. "Or funny!"

"You wanted to know why an anthropologist was assigned to you and I'm telling you what I do."

"Fine then. I'll do the talking," I say, backing down and away. "As I was saying before, Ella invited us over to her house. Well, Ella's mother's dress studio was like — WOW. Sure, they could only afford the worst house in East Rivermoor, but the important thing was despite where they came from before, they were now living in the best neighbourhood…"

"Keep on track, Eliza," reminds Dr Fadden. "You promised me you were going to talk about Ella."

"Oh yeah, *that*," I reply.

"Oh my God," I mouthed.

Behind me Lexi was also staring with her mouth open. I don't think she'd closed her mouth since I let slip about Ella's mum.

Ella finished securing the French doors back against the wall and bounced forward to join us. "Lovely, isn't it?"

"More than lovely!" breathed Lexi.

We stared greedily around the room, trying to take in as much as possible. Both walls were stacked with the most gorgeous fabrics in shelves that rose up to the ceiling. High in one corner a roll of cream muslin had rolled to the floor, leaving a trail like some fantasy spider's thread. The huge bay window bathed the room in late afternoon sunlight, turning everything gold. *Oh yeah*, I had reached the end of the rainbow all right.

Holding court and greeting us like we were royalty, stood two rows of mannequins in the most luscious dresses I had ever seen.

"Go — take a look," Lexi hissed in my ear and gave me a push forward.

"Oh dearest!" came a light girly voice from behind us. "Your friends have arrived and you did not let me know — silly girl."

"I didn't know where you were," whined Ella. "I just wanted to show them your sewing room."

"Silly girl!" repeated Mrs Dashwood breathlessly, as if those words gave her pleasure.

"Mother, this is Eliza and Alexandria."

"Miss Boans," she said and her eyes lit up. "My, aren't you as lovely as your mother herself? The famous Mrs — *Ms* — Electra Boans. I saw your mother in the newspaper last week; she was wearing the most flattering colours."

If I was expecting an OTT fashionista wearing leopard print, I would have been disappointed. Mrs Dashwood was short, ruddy and mousey haired, and not all that notable except for the fact she was wearing some sort of Jane Austen dress in the middle of the day.

"Oh, call me Lizzie, all my friends do."

"Why Miss Boans — *Lizzie* — what a compliment that you bestow such intimacy upon me. I am sure we will become very much acquainted in time. I see you are looking at my recent creations."

Now I've figured out why Ella talks that funny way.

"Yeah. Sure. We can become, um, fully *acquainted*. You really made these yourself?"

"Why yes," replied Mrs Dashwood breathlessly. "Do you like this one? It is only a simple one, an early Regent half-dress. Do you know much about Regent fashion?"

I'm not dumb. I know that a half-dress is a like a regular Armani gown on a local socialite. Full-dress is like an Armani Privé collection gown on an A-list actress walking the red carpet at the Oscars.

"We're studying *Pride & Prejudice* at school?" I suggested.

"Why, what a good girl! My Ellanoir regrettably does not have the head for it. Come with me, I have something to show you that I have not shown anyone else. This way, dear Lizzie."

Mrs Dashwood took my hand and led me to a little alcove on the left side of the room. In the small space underneath the plaster archway rested a bulky expanse of white cloth.

"This is my latest commission. I was hoping that I could show it to someone who might appreciate it a little more."

Mrs Dashwood whipped the cloth away like a magician. Underneath was another dress on yet another mannequin, but — this was the moment I died and moved to a higher plane of fashion consciousness.

The dress was the colour of the sky on a summer's day, when the blue becomes almost white. It was really simple: empire-line, scoop-necked and made as if from one seamless piece of silk. I could just imagine myself in it, the dress fitting like a glove, the soft-as-butter fabric against my skin. It was the most beautiful dress in the world.

"This is what you call Regency full-dress," said Mrs Dashwood knowingly, "but for the contemporary woman."

"You don't say!" I made googly eyes.

"This one has been commissioned by an actress currently starring in a popular soap opera, although for confidentiality reasons I cannot reveal her identity."

I wondered if I was allowed to touch it, the dress belonging to some soapie poptart and all. Behind me, Ella and Lexi were clustered around a mannequin wearing a pale pink dress. Mrs Dashwood looked up and saw Marianne standing by herself on the other side of the room.

We'd forgotten all about Marianne. We couldn't believe it when she agreed to tag along. Funnily enough, the words Dot & Dash had changed her mind.

Marianne was standing in front of a white dress so delicate that you could see the black velvet of the mannequin underneath. Diaphanous and elegant. Just like Marianne herself.

"This is a mull dress in the neoclassical style," explained Mrs Dashwood. "The whitework embroidery — tambour, French knots and satin stitch — is all done by hand."

"This is so beautiful," said Marianne softly. She reached out to touch the front of the dress.

Mrs Dashwood bent down behind the mannequin and fluffed up the small train.

"I am so sorry, dear, this one has already been sold. Or else I would ask you to try it on for yourself. Oh — I am afraid Ellanoir has not yet introduced us. You must be Jane."

The serene look on Marianne's face faded. She dropped her hand away from the dress.

"Sorry, you're mistaken. I am Marianne Jones, Mrs Dashwood."

"Oh, Marianne!" exclaimed Mrs Dashwood. "Silly me! How ever many new friends my little girl has! Please accept my most sincere apologies."

"That's fine," replied Marianne softly.

I know what makes Marianne act so funny at any mention of Jane Ayres, but we never talk about it. Marianne believes some things are best left buried in the past, where they belong. My thoughts were interrupted when my phone rang.

"Hello? What are you doing back—? Fine. Bye."

I tapped Ella on the shoulder.

"I have to go."

"Go?" repeated Ella with a confused expression. "But we're having so much fun!"

"Well, what a shame. I'll see you at school tomorrow. Say thanks to your mum for letting us come over, okay?"

I kissed Ella on the cheek and headed quickly for the stairs.

"But we haven't had afternoon tea and Mum's little cakes yet!" Ella's voice echoed after me.

◆❖

"Thanks."

I make a conscious effort to be polite as the waitress plonks my burger and chips in front of me and passes Dr Fadden's plate to him over my head.

I pick up one of the chips and sniff it gingerly.

"Do you think they use olive oil? It better not be animal fat. Lenworth Henry's brother worked at a fish and chip store once, for community service — *long story* — anyway, overnight the frying oil would harden into this huge block of lard and the next day they would melt it and use it again."

I pop the chip into my mouth.

"You sure have plenty of stories about other people. Makes me think that you'd rather not talk about yourself."

"I love talking about myself; it's not like I'm not self-absorbed, is it?" I say and then I pause and nothing more comes out.

"Come on. Tell me something about yourself that's not on the files they've given me."

"What? Like what music I like?"

I stiffen up because I'm scared he's going to launch into a discussion of what is "trendy".

Dr Fadden swallows his glass of wine in one go.

"Sure. I read an article recently that said people over the age of 35 don't listen to pop music. I think I defy that stat — I mean, I watch Channel V and I like the Top 40."

I cringe, but I look his face up and down. "That's definitely a lie," I say.

"And so you have me there. I like the old time stuff. The real rhythm and blues, not that stuff they call R&B these days with the gangstas and the homies."

I cringe some more.

"In fact, I think my favourite song is *Devil With the Blue Dress.*"

He looks at me when he says that. I look down at my blue trench coat.

"They try to steer you toward doing forensic anthropology

if you choose to study it so that you can become useful as a crime scene investigator — but I find the social anthropology, the stuff that says there's a devil inside of all of us, more interesting. Maybe more insightful."

He sighs wistfully. *Enough of that.* I reach over, take his wine glass and plonk it on the empty table behind me so he won't be tempted by a refill.

"So where are you going after here? Catching up with that 'female colleague' you mentioned earlier?"

"I am going back to my office to type up my notes," replies Dr Fadden. He doesn't answer my second question.

"Is that back in the police station?"

"No."

"What about me?"

"You're going back to the police station."

"No!"

"If the parents of the children at your school could see you now, out of your holding cell and having the freedom to pick out your tomatoes like that, what would they think?"

"I hate tomatoes," I reply, removing a slice and sticking it on the edge of my plate. "And don't pretend this is some fancy restaurant. I don't care what they think. They don't know the whole story."

"Then you better keep talking. You haven't told me, for instance, why you have refused to see your mother since you've been here. Or the lawyer she's hired for you. Do you even realise how much you self-sabotage?"

ry

"I'd rather face the consequences than watch my mother pathetically try to save her reputation," I reply. I press my burger down and cut it in half. "Actually, I'd like to see her reputation go down. Who is the lawyer anyway?"

"Nova Devangari."

"Lipstick lesbian."

"She's one of the best defence lawyers there is. And she likes to take on the sympathy cases to bolster her public profile."

"Exactly what I just said. And I am not a *sympathy case*."

"I don't know, Eliza. I think you might be trying to make me feel sorry for you. Because otherwise, you would have stopped talking by now, and you'd be as good as guilty. And I don't believe you are simply *just guilty*. Even you don't believe so, Eliza. I know that."

"Whatever," I say and I look down at my plate.

Dr Fadden sits stonily in front of his uneaten dinner.

"They have set up an temporary office for me back at the station. I can work from there if I have to."

"If you don't go I will promise to keep talking."

"You keep talking and I will think about it."

◆❖

When I got back from Ella's house, the beige-coloured Mercedes with the vanity plate that reads YES MAN was parked on the driveway, screaming "look what I got from the divorce!" to the entire street. Inside the house, the Gucci handbag on the coat-stand was now joined by a Louis Vuitton suitcase and overnight bag underneath.

"Mum?"

A plastic bag full of white cardboard boxes stood in the middle of the dining table, along with three unopened bottles of wine. They looked sleek and dangerous. Like bullets.

"In here, honey."

I followed the voice to the kitchen. There was my mother, opening the wine-glass cabinet in the kitchen. Fluid in her black jersey dress — Armani, of course — and towering in a pair of Cavalli four-inch leopard heels.

Everyone says that we look the same. I don't think so. She wears her hair curled and chin-length — my hair is long and straight. She has her highlights done by some hairdresser in King Street who apparently does the newsreader's hair on channel seven — our hair hasn't been the same colour for the last twelve years. It's as if she is purposely trying to distance herself.

Lexi says that we can pass for sisters, but I don't want a best friend or confidante. I want a mother.

"I got some takeaway for our dinner from that new Japanese. I thought we could stay in. You didn't want to eat out, did you?"

"No." I replied. "It's a school night."

My mother catches her beautiful reflection in the glass splashback. The beautiful reflection frowns.

"There's streaks on this. That serv — *cleaner*, and the

amount I pay her too! You just can't get decent paid help these days. They all seem to want a whole lot more to do a whole lot less…"

"I messed that up," I said. "In case you've forgotten, I've still been living here while you've been gone."

"Oh," replied my mother.

She went back to opening her wine bottle.

"I am going to talk to her anyway. Why I have a cleaner coming on a Sunday, I have no idea. How is anyone supposed to relax when there's a cleaner bloody banging about?"

I was tempted to remind her that she'd spent the Sunday just past on the other side of the country, but I held my tongue.

"How was the business trip?" I asked instead. "I thought you were supposed to be gone for two weeks? But you're back already."

"Oh yeah, the business trip," said Mum. She beamed her large, fleshy smile at me. "Would you like a drink, honey?"

"No," I said. "I am not old enough to drink. It's against the law."

"Rubbish. Kids in Europe drink red wine."

"We are not in Europe."

"Well fine, little Miss *Provincial*. Suit yourself."

My mother sidestepped me with her generously filled glass.

"It wasn't really a business trip."

"What?"

I followed my mother as she clicked her heels into the living room.

"It was more a *pleasure* trip."

She plonked herself onto the white couch. Drops of wine from her overfilled cup dotted the white linen.

"I'll go get a sponge," I said and turned around.

"No, leave it," she replied. "Don't worry honey, we'll get it re-covered. I am so bored with this couch anyway. Sit down, why don't you?"

I sat down on the white leather Barcelona chair.

"I went with Peter McDoherty."

"McDoh— *eww*. Isn't he like fifty years old? And more importantly — isn't he married?"

"Technically, yes. But—"

"*Technically*? No wonder no one trusts lawyers. Just look at you mum! Y'know what? I reckon you're such a committed divorce lawyer 'cos you're still cut up your own marriage failed!"

"You *did not* just say that!"

"Yes, I *did*!"

My mother smiled at me. I knew exactly what that look meant. It's the one thing I did inherit from her.

"You may not know this because — *surprise, surprise* — I wanted to protect you, but your father wasn't an angel either, honey. The truth is, he didn't leave me — I kicked him out."

"And why was that?" I scoffed back.

"I don't think it matters anymore," she replied and her

eyes glazed over slightly. "If you only stopped thinking of yourself for one moment in your precious little life, then you might actually figure it out."

I hated when my mum became like this: drunk. I was so fed up with her.

"By the way, thanks honey for asking me how I'm feeling," she continued, sarcasm thick in her voice. "There's no need to worry. The trip ended early because it turned sour. I'm okay about it."

"If that is all then I am going to my room," I said and went to stand up.

"Nuh-uh. Sit down."

I sighed loudly.

"Lets have a little grown-up chat."

My mother leaned in closer to me so that I could see her pretty green eyes and smell the alcohol on her breath.

"If I recall correctly, I had a conversation with your principal just last week, y'know, about that naughty thing you did? He asked me what punishment we should give you. I told him to sort it out himself. After all, why else am I paying him thousands of dollars?"

"That's right, I had to do a week of canteen duty with Mrs Wally. Mummy, it was so horr—"

"It's too late to try and *Mummy* me. As I was saying, I left the punishment to Principal Hollerings, but now I think I've changed my mind."

"What?"

"I am punishing you right now, *Eliza Roberta Boans*. You are effectively banned from attending the end-of-school ball. Okay, that's it. You can go running off to your room now."

"What? No! You can't! Marianne is the head of the Ball Committee and Lexi is going to be Belle of the Ball — they're my best friends and I have to be there for them, you don't—"

"I said *that's it*. You wanted a bit of law and order and now you got it. This matter is non-negotiable."

My mother relaxed into the couch and took another sip of wine.

"Fine!" I said to her as my parting words. "If you want to be vindictive instead of fair then do it! Go ahead and punish me for telling the truth!"

I grab a random white box off the dining table as I stormed across the hall toward the staircase. I may have been full of anger, but my stomach was empty. And dinner smelt excruciatingly good.

At the top of the staircase, I watched my mother. With the glass of red wine still in her hand, she steered herself toward her briefcase, grabbed a fist full of papers and went back to the living room. There on the couch, she drank her wine and worked. That is my mother's way of coping.

I remembered the first time I heard my parents arguing. As a five-year-old, standing where I was right now. That's when my mother started drinking. That's when dad started coming home less, until one day he never came back at all.

He said to her, "You know I'm not so much her father as you are her mother."

Huh. If only Dad had tried a little harder, maybe I would be with him instead of stuck here. If only my mother hadn't been a bitch and driven him away and left him with no choice when he had done nothing. But now that my father has that new wife and new family in America, I guess that's all ancient history. There's no point wallowing or even thinking about it.

Up in my room I could see my beloved ocean; I was the tallest thing in East Rivermoor. I thought about how I only needed to jump out one of the windows to be free. From that height I would break every bone in my body. It made me feel better.

The box turned out to be teriyaki chicken. There was no rice and no chopsticks, but I didn't care. I ate it with my fingers sitting on the window ledge, contemplating, well, life. Letting the breeze freeze away the feeling on my face.

I loathed the idea of having to speak to my mother the following day, but she made it easy for both of us. She went to stay in a hotel in the city for a week. She said she was working on a difficult case and needed to be close to work, but we both knew she was only telling half the truth. After she came back, we had both cooled down and gotten over it. Not that I see much of her anyway, even when she is home.

five

I wake up in the doctor's office at the station. My eyes flicker open and I pull myself off the disgusting brown velour couch. It is dawn; I can still see the faint outline of the moon outside the barred window; it chills me to the bone.

The sound of a throat clearing makes me turn around. The door on the cheap cupboard behind me is open. Dr Fadden is standing in the middle of the dark office in fresh clothes, putting on a tie. Or should I say, *trying* to put on a tie.

"Here, let me do that," I say and I brush his hands aside. I have to stand on my tippy-toes, and it's hard trying to keep balanced when you've just woken up and had, like, *carbs* for dinner, but my handiwork is perfect. Just like my so-called-life.

"See? Interest in fashion is good for something. I reckon I'll make a decent enough wife for someone one day."

"Thanks," Dr Fadden replies, sounding somewhat unconvinced.

"Just look at you. Don't you look great when you put in a little effort?"

He doesn't reply. I fiddle with his tie nervously.

"You look like my friend Neil," I blurt out. I instantly regret it.

I watch as Dr Fadden's fingers move across the desk to where his leather notebook is lying open. The flickering computer screen lights his face and out of the shadows he no longer looks like anything but another person who would let me down.

I turn my back on him and rip off the gross trench coat. Underneath the dried blood on my blouse has turned almost black.

Afterwards, when we all went back to my house, all I remember is crawling into bed. I didn't want to shower. All I cared about was Lexi. She lay next to me sleeping so peacefully. I remembered the time when Lexi couldn't wait to wash the evidence off her; this time she wanted to wear it.

Like a battle scar. Like a trophy.

"So why are you all dressed up? Are you going on a lunch date?"

"I am going to meet your mother," Dr Fadden says flatly.

"Oh." I purse my lips. "Why's that? So you can bitch behind my back? So she can confirm what you already know about me? That I'm difficult, stubborn and completely unreasonable?"

"Your words, not mine," Dr Fadden replies. "Let's go."

He ushers me out and down the hall. Unfortunately halfway down the stairwell, we come face to face with Dr Fadden's porn-stached boss.

"Fadden!" growls the chief, but he looks at me instead.

"I'm just taking her back to the questioning room, sir."

"I was under the impression that her holding cell and the questioning room are on the same floor?"

Dr Fadden's face gives nothing away. I look at him eagerly to see how he gets out of this one.

"We came from my office upstairs. Now if you'll excuse me."

"Why is this girl still wearing the *evidence*? Get the clothing bagged now! Fadden, if I find your incompetence has contaminated the evidence, I'm going to send you straight back to the pseudo-voodoo-sciences you came from."

"*Hello*," I emphasise. "I'm here you know. And what am I supposed to wear instead? I don't really want to change into something *generic*."

The chief leers at me. "You want to know what I think? I think you need to be shown how to shut that little mouth of yours. If there's no available clothes I don't care if I have to throw you naked into a cell."

I push past him and run down the stairs. On the landing, under the green exit sign, I stop. I wait patiently for Dr Fadden to catch up. Then I vomit.

"What's the matter?" asks Dr Fadden. He puts his hand on my shoulder.

"Nothing," I say and I push away his touch. I look at the expression on his face. He's trying to do it again. *Know* me.

"What are you staring at? Are you going to write this down in your book as well?"

"Let's get you out of here," he replies. "I'll get the cleaners later." He pushes open the exit door and we both stumble out.

I wrap my arms around me. I am wearing my school uniform for godsake. Not some slutty outfit. Why then do I feel that he has gone right under my skin?

First I start to feel cold. I shiver and my teeth start to chatter. Then I find that I can't breathe. I feel like I am going to die.

Dr Fadden looks into my face. Then he strips off his jacket and throws it over my shoulders.

He hurries me down the hallway. We reach the questioning room and Dr Fadden pushes me onto a chair.

"I think I'm going to die," I gasp.

Great. Wouldn't they just love if I died right now?

"You are not going to die," replies Dr Fadden. "You are just having a panic attack. Put your head down between your knees."

"Put my what *where?*"

"Just do it."

After a while, from somewhere between my knees, I say, "I thought I'm supposed to breathe into a paper bag."

"Does it look like I have a paper bag?" comes the response.

I lift my head slowly back up. "I think I feel better now," I say.

"That's good—"

I go to take his jacket off. He stops me.

"Eliza, tell me about what happened just then."

"I vomited. Is that a crime?"

"I think something hit a nerve just then, in that stairwell with Chief Bullen. Tell me about it."

I'm tired. I've been here for such a long time.

Holding cell, questioning room, holding cell, questioning room, lawyer knocking, mother knocking, questioning room, the chief—

I'm so tired, here in my head.

"You have spoken a lot, Eliza. But you haven't told me a single thing."

I look away from him. He's getting too bright to look at. Kind of glowing with a rainbow halo. Maybe he's an Angel after all, here to judge me and then send me to Hell. He's so distant, all fuzzy around the edges. Yet so close, his jacket wrapped around me.

"Eliza, I'm the only person you haven't turned away since you got here. Please, open up to me. I know you want to talk to someone. Can't you make that someone me?"

Dr Fadden. *Brian.* The only person who has been kind to me. Doesn't act like a pervert, took me out for dinner, let me sleep in his office. Lent me his jacket when I got cold. Dr Fadden who is kinda mean, come to think of it. Who makes fun of me at my expense; who is only doing his job, getting paid, trying to prove something to his boss. Who asked me why I think I vomited.

"Don't you have to be somewhere with my mum?"

"That can wait."

"Good. She would stand you up for at least an hour anyway. Someone should stand her up for once."

I think I have reached the middle of me, my hard stone pit. It might have just left me nowhere else to go.

"Eliza, tell me about Alexandria."

Why do we have to do this again? I have already told him about Lexi. How Lexi once lived on diet coke. I thought she was stupid to think "diet" meant it would make her skinny. But Lexi told me that in her head she imagined it coursing through her body, her bones slowly corroding and collapsing into her bloodstream, being carried away like waves carrying pieces of a cliff back to the sea. Then someone told her diet coke was carcinogenic and she freaked out over *that*.

That is Lexi, I wanted to tell him. That is such a totally Lexi thing.

But Dr Fadden doesn't want to hear stuff like this because he doesn't care about the person she is. He just wants to know about the person he thinks is a cold-hearted killer.

"I told you, it's not Lexi's fault. If you found her fingerprints on the knife it's because she was trying to shove it away from her! Why did you let Ella go, Ella has as much to answer for as—"

"Eliza, listen to me. I *know* about what happened to Alexandria. Talk to me, Eliza. You know I will understand and that I will do something about it."

I start panicking because the rainbow glints and the fuzzy corners I'd been seeing around Dr Fadden suddenly collapse. It takes me a while to realise that tears are falling down my face. Yes, Eliza Boans is bawling her eyes out. *I know*. I was, like, totally not expecting it either.

A white handkerchief swims in front of me. An embroidered letter 'B' is attached to that handkerchief which is attached to the hand of Dr Fadden. I take it and blow my nose.

The doctor comes over to my side and hugs me.

Oh. WTF Brian? That is so…that's nice, actually.

It's not even like Lexi was wearing a slutty dress. Like when Tori said that she dared to wear a slinky red thing. Lexi wore blue jeans and a nice black top that had little black sequins. Sure, it had spaghetti-straps, but hey, it was a hot spring night. And there was me wearing a top that had no sleeves at all. It was me who was even wearing a push-up bra. Not Lexi. And I was safe. I was fine.

◆❖

"It is not about Ella, is it Eliza?" asks Dr Fadden. His voice is not hard or sarcastic. If I didn't know better I would have mistaken it for understanding, and I would have gladly taken it.

Dr Fadden wants me to tell a short story. But it's not that easy. If I just point my finger and shoot down each of my friends in turn, I would make them criminals. These girls are not faceless scum that can just be thrown away. They are my friends and they have blood running through their veins. Just like I have blood in my veins enough to love them.

"Why don't you tell me a bit about yourself, Eliza?"

"It was me," I reply. "It's true. It was all my fault."

◆❖

"Guess what? The school library has burnt down," said Lexi.

"You've got to be joking! How come I haven't heard anything about it?"

I took out my copy of *Pride & Prejudice* and placed it in the middle of the desk, same equal distances between the two of us as I've been doing, for like, *always*.

"I correct myself — the library is, as we speak — in the process of burning down."

"How can the library burn down? Isn't it made out of metal and glass?"

"Honey, the library is full of highly flammable objects," replied Lexi. "Maybe you've even heard of them. They're called books?"

I ignored her. "Who told you this?"

"They did," replied Lexi. Marianne and Neil walked through the door at that moment, ushered in by our English teacher.

"Morning, lovely people," announced Mr Steele. "As you *may* have heard, the library is currently on fire. We have two guests in our class today. Unfortunately their teacher, Professor McFarlane, was deep in the bowels of the library retrieving an ancient and very valuable periodic table when the accident occurred, so he is currently being treated for smoke inhalation. Not to worry. Professor McFarlane, as those close to him — or those that fear him—"

Knowing laughter rippled nervously through the class.

"—may know, is a lot tougher than to let a mere puff of smoke get the better of him. I have agreed to let his small class, who are incidentally both my students in the next period, sit in for a double class of English Lit. So suffer to them!"

The class laughed again. Marianne looked mad, then embarrassed. She pushed me to the side and I watched, unimpressed, as she deposited my bag onto the floor and parked herself on the spare seat instead.

Lexi and I sit on adjoining desks right at the front of the class, butting onto Mr Steele's desk. We've always sat here. I was not ashamed to admit that I loved English Lit. And I knew that I was one of Mr Steele's favourites, so even better.

Neil made a "V" sign in the air to a round of applause, as he headed up to the back of the class. He's recognised his blond jock friend, Alistair Aardant. If Neil thought he was a rock star, then he's the skinniest rock star I have ever seen, with no ass to speak of whatsoever.

On my right, Lexi had draped herself over the back of my chair and pretended to look at Neil while she checked out Aardant. I'd heard rumours that Aardant might be Beau of the Ball this year, so maybe she was hoping he would ask her to be his partner — rather than, say, his *girlfriend*.

"I don't know what Neil and Aardant see in each other." I realised too late I wasn't just speaking in my head.

"Alistair will always be Neil's best boy-next-door even though Alistair's parents moved house, like, ten years ago," said Lexi and she grinned. "What? Jealous much?"

"Grossed out much," I replied. "I heard a rumour they regularly hang out together in Aardant's room writing emo poetry."

Lexi's face went all dreamy as if she was imaging Aardant writing emo poetry for her, so I made a face and left her at it.

"Okay class, please," instructed Mr Steele. "Let's get back to the learning at hand."

"Can we go see the fire, sir?" piped up a voice from the back. I turned my head around, as did most of the class. It belonged to the guy sitting on the other side of Neil. What's-his-face with the black hair and boots, who thinks he's some sort of Punk or Goth or whatever. He just looked like a giant spider to me.

"No, we cannot *go and see the fire*. It is not some spectacle for you to enjoy."

"But sir, shouldn't we go and see if they need any help?"

"With what exactly? With your massive muscles, Mr Gauntly?" replied Mr Steele, pulling his shoulders into a dramatic shrug. "They do have people helping right this instant — they're called fire fighters."

"What if we need to be evacuated? We could be in danger, sir."

"We are not in danger," sighed Mr Steele as he locked his hands behind him. "The library, must I remind you, is isolated on the other side of the school lake. Now, in the unlikely event that the fire somehow manages to burn itself across half a kilometre of water, I am sure we will be alerted."

"But sir—"

"Oh, Gauntly, why don't you just shut up? Let's just get on with the class!"

Marianne and Lexi both turned to face me. Mr Steele turned to face me. The whole class turned to face me. I realised, with a strange burning sensation, that it was me who had spoken.

A black look crossed Gauntly's face. His lip curled into a snarl.

"Settle down, teacher's pet," he spat. "Do you hear me, you stuck-up lot sitting at the front? Little cheerleaders putting on a routine."

I stared at him with loathing choking in my throat. If only his face was close enough to connect with my fist I would, like...

Neil elbowed Gauntly.

"What a tool!" I turned to Marianne, but I found that she was already staring at me. And it wasn't pretty. Marianne was staring at me with a look of contempt.

"What?" I mouthed. But Marianne turned away silently and faced the front of the class instead.

"*Enough,* Mr Gauntly," warned Mr Steele. "Never use such words toward a lady. As I was saying, the matter is settled, and I do not want to hear any more. If you wish to bring your sandwich and watch the disaster during lunchtime, then that is your own time to waste. Now—", Mr Steele strolled slowly to the front of the classroom, "—which of my two favourite students will lead the first reading?"

Hang on. *Two* favourite students? When had there ever been two favourite students?

I forgot that there were two extra students in our class today. And that one of them was sitting beside me right now, squeezed uncomfortably close against my arm. It suddenly became apparent that this special spot in the room, right in front of Mr Steele's desk, was not just my desk for Lit class.

"Miss Jones," announced Mr Steele with a flourish of his hand, "please continue with where we last left off."

Did I hear that right? He just chose *Marianne*.

I thought this was supposed to be *my* class. Marianne is good at everything. English Lit is supposed to be my thing. It is the only thing I'm good at. What with my talent at turning every conversation with my mother into an argument and my ability to repel my dad — it's the one thing I have.

I had to believe Mr Steele was just being polite to Marianne, the *guest*. I couldn't take it any other way. It would kill me.

I pushed the novel, perfectly balanced between me and Lexi, toward Marianne.

Marianne stared down at the novel. Then she pushed it back to me. She reached into her bag and took out her own heavily dog-eared copy.

"—*That the Miss Lucases and the Miss Bennets should meet to talk over a ball was absolutely necessary; and the morning after the assembly brought the former to Longbourn to hear and to communicate*," Marianne read. "'*You began the evening well, Charlotte', said Mrs Bennet with civil self-command to Miss Lucas. 'You were Mr Bingley's first choi—*'"

"'—*Yes; but he seemed to like his second better,*'" I said loudly.

The class was quiet.

"Miss Boans," said Mr Steele. "This is a reading, not a two-way combat. Please wait your turn."

I felt my face flush. But I wasn't sorry. I was only sorry that Mr Steele didn't choose me.

We were interrupted by a knock on the door. Mr Steele went over to answer it.

On my left, a glowering Marianne opened her mouth to say something to me, but I pretended I was suddenly fascinated by a passage in the novel.

"What's wrong with you?" Lexi whispered loudly.

"Nothing," I snapped back. "What's up with you? Upset that I'm ruining your chances with boy-toy up the back?"

Ouch. Even that one managed to flick me in the face and sting.

Lexi went to say something back, but I ignored her. She looked away, upset, and started rummaging in her bag, presumably looking for her imaginary copy of *Pride & Prejudice*.

I felt a tap on my shoulder. Cathy-Ann Moss, sitting directly behind me, was holding out a folded piece of paper between her fingers. When I took it from her, she put her head down immediately and pretended to be writing notes.

I looked at the creased piece of pink paper. I opened it in my lap under the desk.

"Listen to this girls. Looks like Bottle Blonde number two is throwing a party."

Neither Marianne nor Lexi looked at me. They were both still too busy trying to be upset with me.

Bottle Blonde number two, AKA Jane Mutton, was the other half of the Jane Blondes. She was as her name suggested — an overdressed designer spring lamb. We're talking two sizes too small, two seasons too late and *always* a shade of pink. I vaguely remember a glasses-wearing, pig-tailed brunette from Year Eight, but ever since Jane Mutton got adopted by her Bo Peep, that girl hasn't been seen since.

I looked over at Marianne. Back in the beginning of time, Jane Mutton was not Jane Ayres' first choice when she was looking for a BFF. It was no secret who her first choice was. She knew it; everyone knew it.

Unfortunately, the only person who didn't want to know about it was Marianne herself. Jane Ayres may be the biggest bitch this side of the border and always used to getting what she wanted, but she was no match for Marianne.

All I know was that it only took one lunch break, one girl's bathroom, the two of them locked in it, some audible snippets of a heated discussion, and that was the end of *that* plan. Neither Marianne nor Jane ever spoke about it again and everyone was too scared to ask.

In so many ways I could see how Marianne was identical to Jane Ayres. I sometimes wondered why she chose to be friends with us instead. Why she chose to be friends with *me*.

My eyes flicked back to the long, wonky list of scrawled names. Everyone knew that it was Jane Ayres' birthday on Saturday — I mean, how could you not with the way she'd been carrying on? But would it kill the girl to have some nice invitations and RSVP cards made up? Guess she didn't want there to be any evidence. It was also no secret that Jane Mutton's parents were going away that weekend.

I scanned the names. Not that I was eager or anything... and there it was. *Neil*. Under Aardant and Gauntly's names. All three names were written in the same sick-looking handwriting that belonged to the same sick-looking owner.

Great, I thought. *Maybe we can triple-date.* The Jock, Boy-Next-Door and Burberry Trench Coat Mafia. Who in the real world would have nothing in common, except here they have to play pretend because all their dads are on the executive committee of the East Rivermoor Golf Club.

"The party's this Saturday night. I'll put us all down," I said and smiled cheerfully to my left and then to my right. "You can both come over on Friday night and we'll decide on outfits. My mum's brought heaps of clothes back for me from her trip and I'm even going to share. Won't that be fun?"

I didn't get an answer from either, so I scribbled our names onto the pink piece of paper and shoved it into the pocket of my blazer.

I've since spent countless sleepless nights thinking about that one piece of paper. Baby pink and innocent looking, crushed between my lip-gloss and a square of bubble gum.

On it, the lives I was about to sign away. In my girly, loopy handwriting.

If only I hadn't been trying so hard to fight with Marianne and prove she wasn't the boss. If only I hadn't been trying to show Lexi that I was the one in charge. And trying to show Ella how cool my group was. We could have been safe.

I mean, we don't even like Jane. *Either* of them. We would all be whole and not in a million little pieces like we were to become.

◆❖

I found Jane Mutton in the hall after English. She stood in front of me like a little pink elephant, her school skirt so tight that it looked like it had been sprayed on. Which, by the way, wasn't a compliment.

"We'll all be there," I said and I held the note out to her.

"Great!" she replied breathlessly and then she lowered her tone. "This is not *me* saying, right? But if you, uh, want to bring alcohol, then, uh, you can."

I screwed my face up at Jane Mutton's school shirt with its buttons gaping around the bulging contours of her body.

"Um, yeah. See you Saturday night."

◆❖

In my head, I watch that same scene over and over again. My hand with the pink invitation. Jane's fleshy hand, with its pink gem-stoned rings, as it closed tight with the invitation inside.

Too late to take back now.

On Saturday we would all head off in our best outfits to our tragedy. Because I was the leader and I thought I made the best decisions for all of us. It was not Ella's fault.

It was mine, and had been all along.

What a traitor I am.

◆❖

There is a knock at the door.

A slightly thickset, curly-haired girl lets herself in. I'd guess she's in her early-thirties, or as my mum would say, someone in her last year of looking decent before her looks go downhill. I recognise this girl as the youth counsellor that I refused to speak to when I first got here.

She smiles at me encouragingly. I don't smile back. I don't want to encourage her.

"Hey," I say. "Are you the female colleague? The one with the best muffins?"

"Eliza," says Dr Fadden cautiously.

"Brian," she says, turning her eyes on him. "I have some urgent news for you. Regarding one of the other girls."

"Yes?" says Dr Fadden.

She looks at him expectantly. "I need to speak to you privately."

Her eyes shift back onto me. I narrow mine.

"What does she want to say that I am not allowed to hear?" I demand.

"Eliza—"

"Don't *Eliza* me. You're not my mother. She's supposed to be a counsellor, so why is she trying to hide things from me? She's making me anxious. I might have another panic attack, you know, like *before*."

"Shut up, Eliza," says Dr Fadden. He turns back to the counsellor.

"Go ahead. Tell us both."

She gives me a dirty look. "Well, if you insist. And I have warned you, Brian. The Chief Inspector will not be pleased if I contaminate the interviews and I don't want to be held—"

"—just spit it out, Dr Jennens."

My ears prick up at the sugar tone she uses for "Chief Inspector". Interesting.

She sighs.

"I came here to tell you that one of the girls, Alexandria Gutenberg, has been hospitalised."

"What?" says Dr Fadden.

My mouth drops open.

"She was being interviewed when she smashed a mug onto the desk and tried to cut herself. For her safety we've had her sedated and taken to the hospital until—"

"—hang on, you said *we*, who is *we*? Do you mean *you*?"

"Be *quiet*, Eliza," says Dr Fadden.

The counsellor tries to lower her gaze and appear sorry, but I know she isn't. She's just sorry she majorly sucks at her job.

"She was there when it happened, wasn't she? She's the one questioning Lexi!"

"Eliza, calm down. Stop accusing people without knowing the story."

"You bitch," I shout and I stand up. "What did you do to her?"

The youth counsellor takes a step back and looks around nervously.

"Brian," I say, turning to the doctor, and I march right up to him. "Aren't you going to do anything about her? She needs to be stopped!"

Dr Fadden doesn't answer me. He isn't even looking at me.

"Get some help," I hear him say to the youth counsellor, "I think I can handle this, but just in…"

The voice that comes out of his mouth is all wrong. It sounds all broken. Like a bad connection.

"She has to be stopped! Do you hear me?"

"Eliza. Eliza — stop. You're hurting me."

I stare at Dr Fadden's face. I open my eyes so wide that they hurt. He has long red gashes on his cheek. I look down at my hand. There is blood under my fingernails.

"Oh my God!"

"It's okay, Eliza, just sit back down on the chair."

I can't stop looking at my hands. What do I do with the blood on my fingers? Do I wipe it on my clothes? Do I pretend it's not there, or can I ask for a tissue? I have to think of an answer fast. The blood is drying and my hands are shaking.

"I just want her...I...it to stop."

"It will," he says. "I promise you, Eliza. Just sit back down."

"Don't make them take me away," I say weakly. "I'm not crazy."

"Sit down and I promise you, Eliza."

I look at the doctor. He looks like he's fading away. I wish that he would stay. I feel my knees give way. My bum barely touches the chair when someone lifts my arm up. I look at the man all dressed in white. He injects something into my arm and then I don't remember.

six

It was just a little argument. Only a tiny scratch. By the end of the day it had healed. Perhaps under a certain light it could be found by someone who sought it.

I got to the school gates first that day after school. Lexi and I walked home together everyday too, since — well, forever. Sometimes Marianne would join us. It depended on whether she had one of her endless extra-curricular lessons. You know, the ones she said would make me a more accomplished person. The ones she really meant would make me more like her: perfect.

"Hi Lexi," I said.

Lexi couldn't look me in the eye. She was clutching a copy of *The Dieter's Digest* which had headlines such as "Lose Weight with Fat Blockers" and "The Cheeky Chocolate Diet for Chocoholics". Following two steps behind her was Marianne. Obviously the two of them weren't talking to each other either.

"Do you think I'm a *teacher's pet*?" Marianne demanded to no one in particular. "I don't think I'm a 'pet'. I'm certainly not a cheerleader, that's for sure. I have never once attempted to try out for the Pink Prioriettes. I have no idea why he would think that."

"Are you done?" I asked Marianne.

She finally looked up to flash me a hurt look. She shut up.

"Good. Let's get going then."

"Hey, wait for me!"

We turned our heads at the same time to see Ella running toward us.

Ella walked up to Marianne, threw her arm around her shoulder and whispered something into her ear.

Lexi and I stared at each other in surprise. We leaned in eagerly to see what would happen next. I was kinda hoping to see Marianne punch Ella in the face.

Ella pulled away from Marianne's ear, looked her in the

eye and smiled. Then the impossible happened. Marianne looked at Ella and smiled back.

"Should we tell Lexi then?" asked Ella.

Marianne nodded.

Lexi looked suspicious, but curiosity got the better of her and she ran over to them and pushed her ear up against Ella. She let out a sudden squeal and clapped her hands together.

Hang on. Lexi with a huge smile plastered across her face, and Marianne grinning away like she's got BPD? Ella looking as if she couldn't believe her popularity?

So, finally, the three of them were friends. Guess that's what I wanted all along. Why then was I the only one unhappy about it?

"Should we tell her?" Ella asked cautiously under her breath.

"Uh, no," said Lexi. "It'll be a *surprise*."

Lexi bounced up to me and linked my arm with hers, which was a bit of a change from her emo act before.

"She'll see soon enough."

I allowed Lexi to drag me off. I turned to see Ella extend her arm out to Marianne. Marianne rolled her eyes, but she was still smiling. She slipped her arm into Ella's.

"Where are we going?" I asked Lexi.

"I told you, it's a surprise."

"Well at least tell me in what direction we're supposed to be heading, so you don't have to drag me around like I'm your brand new puppy."

"Ella's house. That's all I can say."

"Does this have something to do with—"

"Shhhh! I said *that's all I can say*. Now just be quiet."

I liked how in East Rivermoor four girls could walk home safe. We've all heard stories about what can happen out there. How girls could be snatched off the streets and never be heard from again. Not until their bodies turn up at the bottom of a ditch. That's exactly what happened one summer. It was a long time ago, but the damage is set so deep I think it will always be here.

She was a Middlemoore girl who had disappeared after coming out of a local hotel, last seen partying, drinking and talking to strangers. Our own Mayor had said "if you go out in the rain, then you expect to get wet." He just meant he didn't care because it didn't happen in our suburb. Nothing happened to the good girls that stayed at home with mum and dad.

That was the first girl. Then three more girls disappeared in exactly the same way and that's when our suburb freaked out. Instead of trying to help, it ended its shaky relationship with Middlemoore. But no one can run away from the ditch. It forms its own deep, natural border. On one side is us and on the other is the Middlemoore train-yard where carriages that break down come to rest forever.

The very edge of East Rivermoor was where we were headed to right now. Yes, we do have a "bad part"; face it, doesn't every suburb? If a natural order didn't exist, how else then would my street be the best? It doesn't mean it's over-run by thugs and you might get shot at if you drive by, it just means the houses are smaller and less nice, like Ella's.

I never liked passing here; it gave me the creeps. But it was the shortest way to Ella's house.

I stared at the billboard standing in front of the ditch. It read: *East Rivermoor — the new face of re-urbanisation*. On it is a picture of a happy family with unusually bright and perfect teeth. I stared at it for a long time, looking at the cherry-coloured graffiti dried on the front. I reckon that if I stared long enough at this place, I could still see the old face of East Rivermoor. And it wasn't so pretty back then.

"Eliza, come on!"

I must have drifted off. In the distance Ella and Marianne were already marching toward the purple house with the roof the colour of a thousand exotic bird poos.

I don't dare look down. What if I see her?

"Stop looking at that disgusting ditch. Like, *eww*. I wish they'd get rid of it."

Lexi grabbed me by the hand and dragged me away.

I wondered if they could, or would, ever get rid of that ditch. If they took it away, what would separate us from them? The people on the other side of East Rivermoor.

Inside Ella's place, it was strangely quiet.

"Where is your mum?" I asked.

"Oh, she's gone out for the night," replied Ella, unfazed. She didn't offer to explain where her mum had gone.

"Right. *Now* can you tell me what's happening?"

I sounded grumpy. I didn't like it when I wasn't in control. I didn't care if I sounded like a sad ungrateful cow.

"Hey, don't be such sad ungrateful cow," Lexi said. "Ella's got a surprise for us. Tell her now, Ella."

"Well," said Ella, bursting with excitement. "My mum has made a dress for each one of us! I mean, I personally think they are gorgeous enough to wear to the ball, but like my mum said, they are only half-dresses. You can all take them home today. For free. They're yours."

Lexi squeezed my arm. "Isn't that exciting, Lizzie?"

I frowned. "I thought I told you I'm banned from going to the ball?"

"It doesn't matter," said Ella. "My mum didn't forget about you. And I think you will especially like yours, Eliza. All of us agreed on the fabric."

"*Us?* When did all of *us* agree on the fabric?"

"Oh, on that day we first came here and you decided to suddenly take off," answered Lexi. "We sat down with Mrs Dashwood and we had afternoon tea, in her *design studio.*"

"We had the scrummiest little petit-fours and *real* English tea in a *real* bone-china teapot," said Marianne butting in. "It was the most elegant thing *ever.*"

"Wonderful," I replied flatly. "Well? Where are these dresses then?"

"Let's go see!" said Lexi, grabbing Ella by the hand and pulling her up the stairs.

Since I had no choice, I followed my temporarily crazed friends. I bet there was a full moon that night.

Now, there are probably only a few things in life that would make a East Rivermoor girl go weak, since we've pretty much seen everything worth seeing. But when Ella opened those French doors, I think I cried a little on the inside.

I can't remember too many moments in my life that have made me for one moment forget about my mother, my teachers, my loneliness, my boredom and my piked-out father. That have the ability to make me just truly, utterly, dizzily happy. Those four dresses on the white mannequin bodies — they came pretty close.

"I guess we'd better try them on," said Lexi, interrupting the silence. "Just to make sure they, um…fit."

Nobody moved. I don't think we could. I looked at the faces of my friends standing beside me. I don't think Lexi was worried anymore that I was a bully. I don't think Marianne cared right now that Mr Steele liked her better than me. And even though it still burnt raw and painful somewhere in the back of my mind, right now I didn't care that Mr Steele liked Marianne better either.

Like a bunch of kids in an egg-and-spoon race, we made a sudden run for it, grabbing the dresses eagerly and laughing as the mannequins crashed onto the ground. We raced down the hall clutching the lush, light-as-air dresses. I don't remember my feet touching the ground at all. We piled into Ella's bedroom together, eager to know if she had a full-length mirror.

Ella was right. I did especially like mine. More than like, I *loved* it. I ran my thumb across the label on the back that read *Dot & Dash*. I ripped off my school clothes and eagerly slipped the dress over my head.

As I stared at my reflection, and I felt myself changing on the spot. I was melting into the sky-blue of the fabric, slowly becoming invisible. I could blow away along with the tiny white and sage green flowers on the print. The fabric smelt like summer and in my bones I yearned for the beach and sand.

Marianne was the second to get ready after me. I watched as she stood in front of the mirror in her dress. In white, Marianne looked like a garden bride. She looked beautiful. She always did.

I helped Lexi zip up the side of her dress. Lexi was in pale pink. She looked so sweet, like candy. Like no harm could, or should ever come to her. I spun her around and stared at her pretty face. Look at her. She's the new Queen of Hearts. She's going to make sure those child-victims of landmines have new legs.

Then there was Ella. Ella in taupe.

Lexi once told me that taupe was the colour of sickness and sadness. That nothing should be the colour of taupe, especially not girls who wanted to be happy. But Ella looked beautiful too. We all did, in that moment — one that I knew could only last inside the life of a bubble.

"Do you have any makeup?" Lexi asked Ella. She didn't look very hopeful.

"Of course I do," replied Ella. "What makes you think I don't?"

"I'm sorry," said Lexi. "I thought with your mother — that she'd rather you pinch your cheeks and rub mulberry juice on your lips."

They both laughed. "My mother doesn't have to know everything, you know," said Ella.

I watched as Marianne twisted Lexi's long dark tresses into a braided bun and then worked her magic fingers on Ella's boofy hair. Ella must have thought she had died and gone to Pretty Girl Heaven.

Maybe one day Marianne will tire of her mother whoring her out to all those extra-curricular classes and run off to Middlemoore to become a hairdresser. I can just imagine a chain-smoking, peroxide-permed Marianne, blue-rinsing Middlemoore grannies.

We all dream about it, sometimes we even talk about it, but I know we will never leave East Rivermoor.

"Okay," I said, staring at the others. "What now?"

We were all made up and had trouble looking each other in the eye. It was like we'd suddenly become shy because we'd suddenly become strangers. I looked out of the window instead and realised that the sky had darkened. We must have spent hours here without realising it.

"All dressed up and nowhere to go,"sighed Lexi.

"Not necessarily," replied Marianne.

She tilted her head to the side and smiled her large smile. Marianne reminded me of a cat. One about to eat a bird.

Looking out into the dusk, I found myself thinking of the dead girl again. I could see her tumbling, hitting the shallow water in the bottom of the ditch. The killer was never caught. One day it just stopped. Everyone breathed a sigh of relief and everything went back to normal. But I wonder if it ever really did. They never removed the six-thirty curfew. Dormant is not the same as stopped.

Marianne was propped up lazily on Ella's bed like she was Cleopatra and half-hoping someone would feed her peeled grapes. She had *that* look on her face.

"Come here Ella, Lexi," she said, lifting a limp hand. "Come over and tell me if you think that this is a good idea."

Marianne whispered something into their ears. She spoke too softly for me to hear, but I thought I heard the word *punish*. When the girls closed their eyes, the colours on their eyelids sparkled.

Ella broke out into a laugh.

"I think that is a superb idea. And I have just the thing."

"Let's go then," said Marianne and she yawned. To show her interest, I supposed.

Okay, so I *get it*. It's great that they're all suddenly BFFs, but I didn't expect it to be at my expense. I didn't like being the victim—

"Follow me," said Ella, and she shot out the door with the other two following eagerly.

I looked around at the room and caught my reflection in the full-length mirror. I looked pale. Even a little sickly. The emptiness made me feel ill somewhere deep inside my stomach, so I left the room as quickly as I could.

I found them inside a closet.

Literally. Trust me when I say that a East Rivermoor broom closet can be bigger than apartments in other neighbourhoods. Ella lit a big pillar candle on an iron stand.

"This is my mother's new project," she said. "Apparently 'Zoo Couture' is the latest fashion with, like, pop stars. They all want to dress up like rabbits and things at private parties. But I'm not allowed to tell anyone about it. Well, I mean I *wasn't* supposed to tell anyone about it…"

Marianne reached out to touch a white mask with a long spiral. She bumped the shelf next to it, which made a creaking noise and wobbled. Then something came tumbling down.

Marianne screamed and grabbed Lexi, who screamed as well. The room was suddenly filled with something floating and white. It was filled with feathers.

"Oh my God, Marianne! I got scared half to death," exclaimed Lexi loudly. Then she started giggling again. Marianne laughed loudly and slapped Ella on the back.

"Do you mind being more careful?" said Ella, with a tone of annoyance.

That was the first time I'd heard Ella annoyed. I wanted to look into her face. To see this new, other side of her. But the room was too dark.

"It's only feathers," said Marianne, catching a handful.

"Yeah, but my mum's going to kill me when she finds out that not only have I let you into her secret room, but that you've messed it up as well."

I liked how Ella used the words *secret room*. Maybe that's where she keeps her Mean Girl, the one that doesn't keep sucking upwards all the time. I reckon if you looked inside me you'd find a cabinet filled with cracked china dolls.

"I'll clean it up," said Marianne. She was serious again. "So what did you want to show us?"

Marianne and Ella stared at each other in the dark.

"This," said Ella and she pointed to a shelf.

There sat four severed white heads. Each one was wearing an identical mask made of speckled brown feathers, wire whiskers and pointed ears. They were cat faces. Where the noses should be sat tiny red ribbon roses instead.

"Perfect," said Marianne and she beamed at Ella with what could have been a genuine smile. Or not. The mask came off its stand and over her face before I could tell.

When we looked at each other again, we realised we were not ladies anymore. Now, we were feral.

"I think there is a mirror up the back," said Ella.

I could only tell it was Ella from the colour of her dress. She was the same height as Lexi, and Lexi was the same height as me. One day I would look back at this frozen picture inside my head and wonder why it was Lexi. What it was that was so different about her.

I knocked a shelf with my shoulder and a white-feathered owl nodded back at me. Pearls and ribboned lace dripped from its empty eyes.

"What's this?" asked Marianne, standing in front of a black sheet. In the dark it shimmered like black water. She gasped and took a step back, treading on Lexi's toes and elbowing me in the stomach.

"Sorry," she said. I looked at her face but in the candlelight I could only see the expression of an immovable cat.

Marianne took hold of the sheet and, with a sharp tug, pulled it away.

We found ourselves staring at the mounted head of a dead wolf.

Marianne screamed. Ella screamed. Lexi and I screamed and we all turned around and start running. Feathers whipped through the small space and flew out from under our feet. The pillar candle blew out.

Ella had forgotten that she was supposed to be discreet. Marianne had forgotten that she had promised to help Ella hide the evidence. We ran screaming down the stairs and out through the front door.

It was Marianne who started laughing first. I thought I was

the leader, but maybe it was at that point that things changed. Marianne laughed so hard she doubled over. And staring at her, a stranger in a Regent dress and a brown cat's mask, we all started to laugh as well.

"Oh my God, how stupid are we?" coughed Marianne.

"But who are we now, really?" sighed Lexi wiping her eyes.

"We are nobody now," replied Marianne. "That's why we can do what we want. Come on, let's go."

"But where are we going?"

No one seemed to hear me. They were already walking off together, so all I could do was catch up. Under the street lamps, our shadows were extra long and almost devil-horned.

It didn't take me long to figure out where we were going. I could walk this journey with my eyes closed, even though I haven't been here for the longest time. How long has it been? Ten years? Longer?

A few times Marianne got lost, but I knew where she was taking us. I knew where she was taking *me*. The lamps seemed to light our way like they already knew. This was the way to Neil's house.

"I think this is it," said Marianne looking up at the large, dark red shape. "Tell us Eliza, are we where we need to be?"

"Yes," I replied stiffly, but Marianne didn't hear me. She was bending down by the side of the driveway and grabbing a handful of stones. She looked up to the window in the loft and she aimed a stone right at it.

"Marianne, what are you doing?" I hissed.

"Wait!" replied Marianne. She lobbed another stone at the window.

I turned around. Behind me, Lexi and Ella stood silently like masked twins.

"I think we should leave," I said to Marianne.

"Hang on. Look!"

A light went on inside. The window was pushed upwards and Neil looked out. He was wearing a white singlet. Inside my mask, I winced.

Neil waved. Marianne waved back. Then she took a stone and hurled it at him. *Hard.* Neil jumped out of the way and the stone disappeared somewhere inside his room. I glared at Marianne. Well, as best I could glare out of a cat mask covering half my face. But Marianne thought it was hilarious. She aimed another stone at him. Neil disappeared inside the room.

"Marianne!" I shouted and I grabbed her arm. "Mari — I don't think this is such a — *aahhh*!"

I screamed as a stream of cold water hit both of us at once. I slid the mask onto my forehead and looked up.

Neil looked down at me in surprise. He was holding a suspiciously empty glass.

"Eliza?"

"Yeah?" I replied, wincing again.

Marianne though, was not finished. She had gone back to the side of the driveway and was picking up more stones.

"What are you doing wandering the streets after curfew?"

"Secret women's business," I replied, looking back up at him. Neil smiled down at me. He dodged to the right as another stone sailed past his ear.

Lexi and Ella appeared to be helping Marianne choose the best stones. They had also pushed their masks up. As Marianne lobbed another stone, the both of them stared at her open-mouthed. I would have sworn they were looks of adoration.

This time the stone hit the glass above Neil's head and there was a cracking noise. I jumped. A light flickered on somewhere downstairs. Neil looked up at the cracked pane and then he looked back down at us again. The four of us stared up at him, frozen on the spot, completely guilty and completely visible.

"What have I done to deserve this attack from you lovely ladies?" asked Neil.

"You should have defended us from Gauntly in English today," said Marianne, with her hand on her hips. "It was very unchivalrous of you to just sit there and let us just take his crap."

Neil looked at the cracked window again and then back to Marianne.

"I'm sorry," he replied. "I won't let that happen again."

From somewhere downstairs in the house, we could hear a man and a woman's voice.

"Okay. Time to leave," said Marianne. She pulled her mask down. Lexi and Ella did the same. Marianne grabbed Lexi's fingers in one hand, Ella's in the other and made a run for it. The light on the front porch flicked on. I gathered up my skirt and turned around.

"Eliza!"

I turned again and looked up at Neil.

"Just want to say," he said, "that you look pretty..."

I bit my bottom lip.

"...strange. But in a good way."

Oh yeah. *Right*. I rolled my eyes. At that moment Mr and Mrs Fernandes appeared on the porch in hilarious, matching dressing gowns.

"I think I looked better before you dumped water all over me," I replied. Neil winked at me. I made a face at him and pushed my mask down. Neil slammed his window and the light went off in his room. I ran after the others into the safe shadows of the street.

Marianne, Lexi and Ella had stopped under a street lamp. They were panting and falling over each other in laughter, masks discarded on the ground.

"Marianne was telling us about what happened in English today," exclaimed Ella. "If only I'd been there, Lizzie!"

No, I don't think so, I thought. *No, you don't call me that.*

"This is the best fun I have ever had," said Ella, still puffing. "I've — never done anything like this before — this is just crazy mad!"

"Well," said Marianne, squeezing Ella's shoulder. "It's because you made the right choice to hang out with us."

"Um, yeah," replied Ella and she put on a bright smile.

"I propose a toast to our new friend," said Marianne. "She's just passed her first test with flying colours."

Lexi was standing there beaming. I thought about giving Marianne a dirty look. I noticed lately that Marianne thought she made the rules. I didn't like it.

"Let's go back and get cleaned up," said Marianne.

"So. You're still all coming over to my house tomorrow night to choose outfits?" I asked, inserting myself between Marianne and Lexi. "Oh, by the way, Ella, Blonde Two is having a birthday party for Blonde One this Saturday. I put your name down to go. Hope you don't mind."

"I know," replied Ella, too quickly. "Um, I've already told her I'll be there."

I raised my eyebrows.

"Good then," I said. "We'll meet after school. Like we did today."

"Ugh," said Ella. "Sorry, can't do. I've promised to be elsewhere."

I felt a drop of water hit me hard in the face. It was starting to rain. There was a rumble in the distance, and it looked like another electric storm was blowing in from the coast. And here we were in our thin dresses, wandering around in the dark. Suddenly I felt vulnerable again.

◆❖

fury

East Rivermoor built a wall to keep the world out. But what if the real danger came from within? Before the seven o'clock news started to call us monsters, I wondered whether deep inside I wanted myself to be one anyway. Neil once told me you had to become a monster so that you didn't become the victim of one instead. I don't care what anyone says. I believe him.

seven

There were two striking things about Friday morning.

The first was that the rumour mill was abuzz with the news that a gang of thugs had terrorised East Rivermoor overnight. I saw Ella out of the corner of my eye as I walked the hall toward the Science Wing for Psychology class. She was huddled up behind a marble pillar with Jane Ayres, talking so fast it looked like she was vomiting. I couldn't hear anything above the noise of the other students. Jane looked suitably impressed with whatever Ella was feeding her, like a mother bird feeding her chick regurgitated gossip.

The second thing was that Marianne looked perfectly normal. Her blonde hair was pulled up in a high bun with a black satin bow, a matching bow at the throat of her perfectly pressed blouse. She sat with the type of posture my mum's always going on about me having, her Psych textbook already opened to the right page. She didn't look like someone who would break the six-thirty school-night curfew. Or someone's window. We sat on high stools behind a sterile white bench, divided by Neil Dennis Fernandes.

"Are the rumours true that your house was attacked last night?" Marianne asked him with a completely straight face.

"Yes," replied Neil. "My parents had to call the police. I mean, our property was damaged and everything. I feared for my life."

The two of them chatted with the ease that came from being each other's only company in Chem four days a week. They seemed to have the comfort level of a pair of siblings. Or, of a pair of soulmates.

Marianne made a *tsk-tsk* noise. "What is the point of having curfews when they are so blatantly flouted? Personally, I blame the parents."

"Oh, I blame the kids," said Neil. "Teenagers just don't have any respect for rules these days. It was completely different in my day, Marianne, during the war. Back then, these kids would have gotten a good flogging."

"Oh, I completely agree," said Marianne without flinching.

◆❖

I used to think Marianne would make the perfect serial killer. I don't think that anymore. Now I know that Marianne can be a victim just like the rest of us.

◆❖

"I heard that they purposely chose to attack you — is that true?"

"They tried to kill me. I had to show the policeman the empty glass with the water I used to try and fight them off. I do believe this is a hate crime, Marianne."

"Did you get a good look at these assailants?"

"No. I only saw shadows. They moved too quickly. Like *cats*, you could say," replied Neil, leaning his chin onto the back of his hand and smiling at Marianne.

"Ah," said Marianne, raising an eyebrow. "What about your parents? Did they see anything?"

"They only saw what looked like a group of three, most likely four, male youths fleeing the scene. That is what I overheard them telling the police anyway."

"Four male youths, did you say?" asked Marianne with a mock tone of surprise. "Now, how many gangs of four male youths exist here? I believe that would be, like, *none*."

What the hell? In case they have forgotten, this is not

Chem with the two of them alone, this is Psych and I am here too. I mean *hello*?

◆❖

"Hello? Can you hear me?"

I can feel a dead weight somewhere at the back of my head. Then I realise that weights are also attached to my fingers, my hands, my arms, my legs — my whole body. So I am not dead. I am horizontal somewhere. I don't want to open my eyes, but I want to know what Hell I've woken up to.

The first thing I see is a bare concrete ceiling. That is all I need to see really. I shut my eyes again quickly.

"Try not to move," says the female voice above me. "If you really have to, do it slowly."

I try to prop myself up onto my elbow. The lumpy surface beneath me sags and groans. I am on some disgusting old bed, in an even more disgusting room. There's a sink, and a plastic chair is squeezed in tightly next to me. The fluoro lighting makes the whole room greenish. When I look at my wrists, I can't see my veins.

How many criminals and druggies and drunks have been here before? Is this where they think I belong now, too?

I look up and see that it's the counsellor who's spoken to me. I want to shout at her to go away, but when I open my mouth my throat is so sore I end up in a coughing fit.

A glass of water is pushed into my hand. I take a mouthful and I want to spit it out onto her face. Eww, *tap water*.

I only force myself to drink it because I'm choking to death.

"Your friend will be fine. She's been taken to a private hospital. Her cuts are only superficial."

"You would know superficial, wouldn't you?" I snap at her.

She looks back at me and bites her bottom lip.

I give her a massive fake smile. I take another drink of the water. I wonder if it's making my insides bleed.

"You can leave now. I want to see Dr Fadden."

She doesn't look pleased, but she knows she can't do anything about it. She's not the boss of me. I'm not as fragile as Lexi. I won't let her do that to me.

The youth counsellor marches out. Her high heels — black strappy things — click against the concrete. My eyes follow them eagerly down the hallway. Wow. Roger Vivier's latest collection. I know because my mum has the exact pair. They cost two-and-a-half-thousand dollars.

You know, I can profile too. One: I don't think this youth counsellor could afford them on her salary. Two: they're the type of shoes a guy would buy a girl.

I almost cry when Dr Fadden appears against the metal bars of the sick room. It's like I'm already in jail and he's come to visit me. I'll do my totally nuts but strangely sexy Angelina-Jolie-from-*Girl-Interrupted* routine, and he'll get me out. I know what he's going to say. That whether I stay here for the rest of my life or whether I walk out is my choice alone. Ha, I reckon I can see through him too.

"How are you feeling?" he asks, pulling the plastic chair up to the bed.

"Worse than ever."

"I am sorry that had to happen."

"Sure you are."

"I didn't want you to hurt yourself. I had to get Michelle to help me."

I stare at the fresh white tape on his cheek.

"Michelle, is it? Not Dr Jennens?"

"Look, if I really thought you were crazy, you'd be strapped down to this bed, you wouldn't be able to slouch like that."

"Who do you think you are, my mother?" I say and narrow my eyes at him. "I didn't call you in here to argue."

"So?" Dr Fadden leans in close to me.

"I'm ready to talk. I'll tell you what happened at the party."

"That's the right attitude, Eliza."

"Yeah. Whatever. The only thing you will have to promise me is that I get to tell it my way, without interruption. Not just the facts I know you want to hear. I'm going to tell it my way."

Dr Fadden looks down at his hands and back up again.

"Of course I'll listen."

"In exchange I want to see Lexi. In the flesh."

He looks unimpressed. He stands up and puts one hand on his hip and the other over his forehead.

"Take it or leave it."

The doctor puts both his hands on his hips. Then he stares at me.

"I saw Neil on Tuesday," he says.

"Don't try and change the subject! Don't you dare try and bring him into—"

"I just thought you might like to know."

"I don't care! I don't frickin care!" I put my face into my palms. What does he think he's trying to do? Break me? Because he's doing it totally wrong.

"Fine, Eliza. It's a deal."

I look up to see his hand in front of me. I don't really want to make the deal anymore. Then I remember that it was me who came up with it in the first place.

I take his hand. It is calloused and rough. I trust him. How can I not? Do I have a choice anymore? I swapped my heart for a bargaining chip a long time ago. And here I am turning it over and over again in my hand, not sure what to trade it in for.

◆❖

"As far as I know, gangs of four male youths do not exist here — isn't that right?" Marianne asked Neil as she leaned in towards him. "See, two isn't enough for a gang and three means a third wheel, but four guys is a boy band, isn't it?"

"Shhhh!" I hissed and shot Marianne a look. If she were sitting directly next to me I would have kicked her.

I glanced behind me to look at Aardant, his mouth hidden

behind his gripped hands. I rolled my eyes at him and he managed to force a smile between his fingers. *Jealous much?* I wanted to say to him in Lexi's words. *You don't know how much*, I answered for him.

Professor Adler entered the room in his lab coat and a black fedora hat. As long as we've attended his classes, the Professor has never done any chemical experiments to need a lab coat. Neither has there been any sun in our basement classroom to need a hat. Even in the middle of winter, the room was warm from the earth pushing in around us. For an hour we would be buried here with no marker or trace.

The Professor was carrying a metal cage in each hand. Each contained a white rat, and there were heaps of wires and things. I had a bad feeling about this. I put my hands over my eyes and looked down at the desk.

"Miss Boans!" called Professor Adler in his hoarse voice. "Would you like to be of some assistance to me?"

I shook my head, my face still in my hands.

The metal cages came clunking down on Professor Adler's demonstration table.

"Now, can anyone tell me what they think we are going to learn today?"

Marianne's hand shot up immediately.

"Miss Jones?"

"I believe it is Learned Helplessness."

"Correct, Miss Jones. Is it because you have read the curriculum?"

"No, sir," replied Marianne, sounding slightly annoyed. "The setup of your experiment is similar to the diagram on page six-hundred-and-fifty-three of our text book."

"Well, my dear Miss Jones," replied the Professor. "I can only give credit to your fine mind."

A look of surprise crossed Marianne's face; she beamed happily at Neil.

"Now class — Learned Helplessness. Page six-hundred-and-fifty-three of your text, as stated by our star pupil. Rather than waste my breath though, on a generation that obviously has no attention span—" Professor Adler flicked Marianne a knowing look, "—I will demonstrate it instead. Now watch carefully, class. See this device I have in my hand? Every time I press the red button, it will automatically administer an electric shock to Rat B."

There was a shuffling and scraping of chairs on the polished concrete floor. I bet everyone was leaning in eager not to miss any of the action. I still had my hands over my eyes.

"I can't watch this," I whispered to Neil. "If I thought Psychology was going to be like this, I never would have picked it."

"What did you expect? That we would all lie around on leather couches talking about our feelings?"

"Er, pretty much," I replied. "How can you bear to watch? Don't you remember *Tacky*?"

When Neil was six years old, he became the proud owner

of a brown rat with a white spot. He named it Ratattack. Neil and Tacky were inseparable; they even slept on the same pillow. When I had to sleep over at Neil's because my parents were going on another marriage counselling retreat, we would drag our sleeping bags together and Tacky would sleep in between us.

One day when we were out on the front veranda, Tacky jumped out of Neil's hand and was never seen again. On the same day Marianne's cat, Mr Darcy, looked much fatter than usual.

"That was a long time ago," said Neil. "We all change. We have to get tougher, don't we? Just watch for a little bit. Just enough so you don't fail next week's exam."

I fanned open my fingers in time to see Professor Adler press the red button down with his thumb. The rat in the cage jumped, then slumped back down. It didn't even try to cower in the corner or anything. It just lay where it was and shivered. I felt a piece of my heart go thump onto the concrete floor.

"Rat B," said Professor Adler tapping the cage with his stick, "caused a bit of a fuss when first administered the electric shocks. Now multiple shocks later, the rat has realised that there is no means of escape. It has basically given up."

To further demonstrate his point, Professor Adler pushed the button again.

I felt sick. I couldn't stop looking at that rat with its beady pink eyes staring straight at me. I just wanted to get away from it. I had to—

"Are you all right?" asked Neil.

"No," I replied. "I have to get out of here."

"Don't move," said Neil.

"But—"

"If you run out of class again you'll be on a one-way journey straight to Hollerings. And since I'd have no choice but to go after you, that will make two of us. Don't know about you, but I don't really want to be doing three back-to-back detentions. Scarily enough I'm starting to become a really good janitor, and if that's the career path I choose, I think my parents will kill me. Stay where you are and I promise I'll put it right. Trust me?"

"Okay," I replied, but I didn't believe him. I realised I was shaking. I was shaking just like the rat.

"Neil—" I said.

"Eliza, can you shut up?" Marianne responded instead. "I know that you don't care if you fail, but Neil and I do."

OMG. I wanted to say something even ruder and smarter back, but I couldn't open my mouth. I was too crushed.

"Compare the response then, of Rat A, a perfectly unaltered specimen not previously subjected to any adverse stimuli."

The Professor lifted the door of the other cage. The rat shot out, ran across the floor and quickly disappeared.

Girls screamed and a few scrambled on top of chairs. On the other side of Neil, Marianne quickly stood up and backed away from the bench. The boys started making brave moves to save everyone from the impending doom. I just sighed.

"Hey, watch it!"

"Why don't you watch yourself!"

Marianne had backed onto Aardant's bench. His open bottle of water was now horizontal and running over his pad of paper, across the now blossoming ink, and onto his lap.

He looked angry. Not just pissed-off angry, but seriously *angry* angry. I thought he might slap Marianne then. And I found myself strangely intrigued about whether it would happen. I have to admit I was a bit curious about finally seeing all that rage and pent-up sexual tension come out.

"Fine. I'm sorry," said Marianne assessing the damage. "Here. I'll help you clean it up."

"Just leave it. I don't need your help."

"Why do you have to be so difficult? I doubt you've been writing legit notes anyway."

"Why do you have to be such a show-off? I doubt you're capable of even forming your own thoughts."

"Why do you have to be such a fu—"

"Jones! Back in your seat." Neil slid his arm across her shoulders and pulled her back in.

That shut her up. And Aardant. And me.

You don't know how much.

"Class!" demanded Professor Adler. "Do not attempt to retrieve the specimen. I will retrieve it myself after class. This rat is on loan to me, please keep in mind it has to be returned to the owner in original condition."

They let us take water into classes. Unlike other schools that might be scared of you, like, doing damage to school property with a bit of plastic and clear liquid, they care about our health here. Ninety per cent of blood is made of water. It only takes two per cent of it to go away before dehydration sets in. But the human body is very resilient. You need to lose over forty per cent of your blood before death starts to set in.

"Now for your last major assignment," announced Professor Adler. "I want you all to document for me a case of Learned Helplessness involving humans. Note, I will not be held responsible if you inadvertently give someone psychological damage. Please take a copy of this release document and pass it along."

I waited in the hallway after class for Marianne and Neil. Everyone had long since raced off. I just *had* to be stuck with the two exceptions to the rule. Marianne wanted to probe the Professor with more questions about the assignment, even though she knew that she would get the top mark anyway.

As for Neil…well you figure it out. Marianne always got what she wanted.

Maybe it's been that way since Neil had that argument with six-year-old Marianne over Mr Darcy's dietary habits, and Marianne won.

Maybe he liked following Marianne around, just like all the boys at school, with poorly rehearsed end-of-school ball invites stuck in their gobs. I mean, I thought Luke Harris, chairman of the Yearbook Committee and sorta good-looking was going to ask me to the ball today, but instead he said, "So, where's your friend Marianne?"

Marianne, who was better than me at everything. I felt sick.

"Here," Neil's voice said.

In his hands, wrapped inside an old cleaning rag, was Rat B. I looked into Neil's eyes. They were black and kind.

"Adler says I can keep him. He was planning to throw him out anyway; he says he's no good anymore. Too much has happened. Adler says he won't live long. But I'll take care of him till then."

I nodded. Neil is a good guy. Neil's promises are good.

"At least I know he won't try and run away like Tacky," he added cheerfully.

I tried to smile, but my heart was broken. I should have said *thanks*, but all I could think of was Marianne. No. I am *not* jealous. Why should I be?

Over Neil's shoulder I could see Marianne standing there, textbooks clutched in her arms, waiting impatiently. When she could feel my eyes boring into her, she turned to face me with her usual look of contempt.

shirley marr

Outside, it's getting dark. The last thing I remember is waking up in the doctor's room. I must have been under for ages. This is *so* killing me.

The doctor snaps the handcuffs on me.

"You do realise I can still knock you over the head with both fists and run away, right?"

"Eliza, I would love to cuff your ankles together, but then how would you walk?"

If I didn't know any better, I would have sworn he thought this was fun.

"I'm taking a huge risk with you, Eliza Boans," says Dr Fadden. "If you are stupid enough to try and run away with cuffs on, trust me, you will be found and dragged back to me like a fugitive. That would be very embarrassing for you."

"Who says a girl with cuffs is a fugitive?" I mutter. "I could just be running away from an adventurous boyfriend."

Dr Fadden laughs. It makes my arms breakout in goosebumps. If I had any hairs on my back, they would be standing up right now. It's freaky. To be talking and making jokes so casually.

The doctor drives an old black station wagon that looks like it's a hundred years old. It is trimmed in silver and has bulgy eyes like a goldfish. It looks like a funeral hearse.

"Family wagon, huh?" I say. "Where's your family then, Brian? Are they with your female colleague? Miss Muffin?"

"Just get in the car," replies Dr Fadden, pulling the passenger door open.

It's become almost a game.

"I'm sorry," I say, as I struggle to wriggle in with my hands bound in front of me. "This car is ancient. It suits you."

"Are you hungry? You want drive-thru?"

"How are you going to explain this at the service window?" I lift my wrists. "Hmm, let me think, stubbled-face guy in a black coat rocks up in a big black car with a cuffed girl in the backseat. Doesn't say serial killer to me at all…"

"You want to eat or not?" Dr Fadden replies. "Then you keep your hands down and shut up."

We travel in silence.

"Sooo…" I say after a while. "You were kinda saying about Neil before…"

"Thought you didn't want to talk about it."

"I don't. But how is he?" I ask and I realise it is the wrong thing to say.

"They went through the usual procedures with him. He's in a safe place…if that's what you're worried about. I can release him to his parents, if you can help me clear him."

I ignore that last part. "Will I be able to see him?"

"Are you trying to make another deal with me?"

"No," I say quickly and I shut my mouth.

"Then it all depends whether you get out or not. So have a good hard think about that."

❖❖

I walked home with Neil and Rat B that Friday after school. I just wanted to talk about Rat B. That's *all*.

"How is he?" I asked.

"More responsive now, I think. I gave him some cheese out of my sandwich at lunch and he ate it."

I looked at the little pink-eyed face staring out of the rag. I looked at the skinny black tie Neil was wearing. It had some sort of watermark pattern on it. I squinted to try and detect a brand. Then there was his black leather belt with the silver square buckle at the front…I realised where I was staring and quickly diverted my eyes upward.

"You know the early bird? Well, I heard you go to bed *before it*."

"Who told you that?" asked Neil with a hint of a smile on his face.

"Oh, just rumours," I replied. "There has been a lot of talk about, you know, the attack on your house last night."

"Well, just because the light is off in my room doesn't mean I am asleep."

"Oh yeah?"

"Haven't you heard the rumour that I'm fairly popular with the ladies of this school?"

"Of course. And I believe I'm staring right at the person who started that rumour. I doubt you were being 'popular' with the ladies though. More like being 'popular' with a comic book under the sheets."

I could still feel his postcard inside the pocket of my blazer.

I'd been meaning to take it out. Seriously…

"Hey, don't hurt my feelings," said Neil. "Comic books rock. I think I'd rather spend my time with one than with any of you vapid Priory girls."

I grinned.

We were standing on the bridge. We used to meet here when we were little. Right in the middle. We liked to watch the yachts sail away. The water is the only other way you can leave East Rivermoor.

The water that day was the same colour as the sky so I couldn't tell where everything started and where it ended. The houses stood in front of us, lined up like debutantes in different coloured dresses, waiting to be asked for the first dance.

"Here, hold him."

"Oh," I said awkwardly, not knowing where to put my hands.

"How do I—?"

"Like this. There you go!"

The wind was blowing pieces of my hair around my face. My hair had a mind of its own, reaching out like fingers toward Neil. I bunched it all up self-consciously. I wished I could do something nice with my hair, like Marianne did with hers. But I wasn't good at much.

"Thanks," I said and I popped the rat on top of Neil's head. Like I used to do with Tacky.

"Hey!"

"It looks great on you. Seriously. It's the latest trend. All the boys in Europe are doing it."

"I think it'll look better on you," he replied and reached for the rat. I pushed it back onto his head and my hand brushed his hair.

"What shampoo do you use?" I pressed his shoulder down and pushed my nose into his black hair. "It smells nice."

"Head and Shoulders? I don't know! Get off me."

"I wanna touch your hair! It's so salon smooth." I rearranged the rat so the front paws went over one of Neil's ears.

"Remind me again, are you turning seven or seventeen this year?" asked Neil.

"I like your hair," I said and I twisted a lock of it between my fingers. "Give me some."

"Give you *what*?"

"Your hair."

"You're a strange, strange little girl Eliza Roberta Boans."

"That's a compliment," I replied with a shrug. My cheeks felt hot. I held Rat B out with both hands like a peace offering. "I just wanna put some of it in a locket and wear it every single day and tell everyone how you're, like, my sun and my moon and that every day without you makes my life ebb away a little bit more…"

When he reached his fingers out, they brushed against mine.

"I'll see you at the party," he said.

"So is that a yes?"

"Yes, as in I'll be there."

"Meet me on the bridge? I'll bring the scissors."

"Goodnight, Eliza."

I stood and watched Neil as he headed up Grovelands. Honestly, I wouldn't have watched. If not for the fact I was looking out for Rat B.

It was then I noticed that Neil didn't go down Southgate to get to his place. He just kept walking. I should have thought about Marianne and what happened with Aardant. I should have remembered how Neil said, "I'm sorry, I won't let that happen again." I should have thought something of it, but at the time, I guess, I was just thinking about the rat in his pocket.

◆❖

"Eliza? I said *Eliza*, what do you want?"

"Huh? Oh. Sorry. Um…a double cheeseburger and large fries. With extra pickle."

I wonder if I should ask for a coke as well. I don't have a calorie counter and don't want to overdo it, just in case.

"So the deal. That's still on, right?"

"I said yes the first time didn't I?" Dr Fadden chucks the brown paper bag at me and drives off.

"You promise you'll take me straight to see Lexi after I tell you what happened? You won't back out?"

"I promise."

"Then here goes."

The party marked the change of many things. The very least being Ella's hair colour.

eight

Curfew on non-school nights and public holidays is a generous eleven p.m. At seven-thirty, one-and-a-half-hours fashionably late, Marianne, Lexi and I walked arm in arm toward Jane Mutton's house.

"So, we're going to Eliza's for a 'study and sleepover' right?" said Lexi.

"Check," replied Marianne cheerfully.

After much prodding, Marianne had finally been convinced to abandon her weekend super-study session to come out with us. After assigning Marianne to what Marianne does best —

organising the present, setting the cover story and generally bossing everyone around — she was even beginning to relish the thought of attending a Jane and Jane party. Almost.

We could see Jane's house before we even neared Southgate. Every light inside had been turned on, and then some. White paper lanterns swayed gently in the breeze, strung out between the old Jacaranda trees. The house was so bright I bet you could probably see it from outer space. Along with the Great Wall and Jane Mutton's humongous ass.

"Very nice," said Marianne. "Jane's gone all out. I hope there's a chocolate fountain."

"Well, she has to doesn't she?" replied Lexi. "I've heard the rumour that this could be her last chance to impress Blonde Number One. Apparently Mutton's *that* close to being ditched."

"Where'd you hear that from?" I asked.

"Oh, from Charlotte Brosnan or one of those girls, I think. Who heard it off someone else who apparently heard it from Jane Ayrehead herself."

"Oh really? How reputable," I said sarcastically.

Lexi shrugged. "Yeah, I'm not really listening to the rumour mill at the moment. I mean, after hearing from Maggy Boyle that a knife-wielding gang robbed Neil Fernandes' home, tied him to a chair and cut off his hair, I've kinda lost my faith in it a little…"

At the mention of Neil's name Marianne giggled and absentmindedly hid her smile behind the Chanel gift voucher she was carrying. I grimaced and stared straight ahead.

For once we were dressed practically for the weather. The first signs of a sticky summer were coming through. When I brushed against Lexi, she was warm.

I remembered how in the winter we would still go to parties in little tops and dresses, our breath hanging in the air. We would walk to where we needed to be with blankets and big jackets, and then hide them in bushes before making our grand entrance. So that it seemed we never got cold; so it seemed we were invincible.

Lexi was wearing a spaghetti-strap top and jeans. A new pair of black earrings she made last weekend brushed against the tops of her shoulders. My casual chick, bohemian baby. She was coughing and said she didn't feel well, but I reminded her it had never stopped her from partying in the past.

Marianne on the other hand was wearing…well, an outfit that seemed to be wearing her. I wondered what her teachers would think of this other Marianne. Not the one who always handed in her assignments on time, but the one in a tight red, blue and white party dress with red footless tights and the tallest purple heels you've ever seen.

I was the only one of us wearing a strapless top. Teamed with a pencil skirt. Only because Lexi said it made me look super sleek. It wasn't like it was slutty or anything — the skirt went past my knees.

"Do you think it's going to rain tonight?" asked Lexi and she sneezed.

"That'll totally bitch the party," I replied.

"Yeah," said Marianne, sounding thrilled. "That'll bitch it."

There were a few people already mingling in the foyer in front of the marble double-staircase. Lexi and Marianne recognised a group of girls from their Art class, who were sharing something blue that I knew wasn't cordial. They wandered over, leaving me to carry the giant tin of fruit salad. Marianne said we should bring something to be polite.

I sighed and rolled my eyes. This was the first time I'd been to Jane Mutton's house. Her parents didn't believe in parties. I guess that's why she was holding one while they were conveniently away.

The Muttons had moved to East Rivermoor five years ago, after they struck it big in the Powerball. My mother calls them *nouveau riche*. They definitely still had more money than taste. There was heaps of granny material and gold urns filled with fake fruit. I thought of my mother's chic white Barcelona chairs and natural linen throws. The Muttons, I guess, decorated their house according to how they thought rich people should.

I turned and bumped right into Jane Mutton, who was wearing the most hideous pink satin dress.

"Hi Jane. Here, this is for you." I shoved the tin of fruit salad at her.

"Uh, thanks," she said. She looked nervous.

"What's wrong?" I asked. "You are the hostess.

So don't look so glum. *Smile*."

Jane didn't look like she was going to smile anytime soon.

"Let's go talk somewhere private," she said, turning around. I followed after her.

In the kitchen, Jane dropped the tin of fruit salad on the bench top and crossed her arms. I looked around the kitchen. It was even more OTT than the front of the house: there was even a freakin' chandelier hanging off the ceiling.

"What have you heard?" Jane blurted out.

"Hey, calm down," I said. "I haven't heard anything."

I opened one of the drawers and rattled the contents, searching for a can opener.

"Cut the crap, Boans," said Jane. "I know you and your friends are secretly laughing behind my back. Now tell me or I am going to kick you out of my party."

I didn't want to be kicked out of this party. I mean, I had taken over two hours to get ready and I wanted at least half the guests to see my outfit before I left.

"Fine. I know all about you and Jane Ayres," I lied, remembering what Lexi had said earlier. "What are you going to do about it?"

"Crap," replied Jane and her shoulders dropped. "So it is true? Janey's going to dump me for Ellanoir Dashwood."

WTF? *Ellanoir Dashwood?* Our Ella? What was this crazy chick going on about?

"Look, I know you and I are far from best friends," said Jane, "but we both know we need to do something about this.

You have to keep Ellanoir in your group!"

Jane's cheeks turned an even more horrible shade of pink than her dress. It took me a while to register the fact that she was asking me for help.

"If Ella defects to Janey…you know what will happen to me. Please Eliza. Who can I be friends with if she ditches me? I'm going to be a complete outcast for the rest of the year and I can't…I can't bear that thought."

"Well maybe you should have tried a bit harder," I found myself blurting out. "Look at your hair. I can see a full inch of brunette root."

I finally found a can opener and I started slicing open the tin.

"But I am," said Jane pathetically, touching the top of her head. "I'm trying hard."

You know, I kinda felt sorry for Jane at that point. I would have given her a hug if we hadn't been staunch enemies. I thought of all the mean and petty things she had done to me over the years, like when she whacked that blue slushie out of my hand and onto my brand new Prada dress. I forced myself not to show any sympathy. On the outside, anyway.

"There's nothing I can do. Sorry," I replied.

I dumped the contents of the can into the punch bowl. I cracked open a bottle of vodka sitting on the bench and poured the whole lot in. Then I walked off. Ella had some explaining to do.

"You have to do something, Boans!" yelled Jane behind

me. "Even if you don't care about me, I know you care about your little group! What will people think if someone you've chosen walks out on you?"

◆❖

Marianne and Lexi were still talking to the Art girls in the foyer. I marched up to them, but someone got there first.

It was Ellanoir Margaret Dashwood, making her grand entrance through the front door.

Average Ella, with average brown hair, average height, and average looks, was wearing the tiniest black dress I had ever seen. I mean, the word *tiny* did no justice to this scrap of material. Ella's hair was no longer average. In fact, it wasn't even brunette. It was platinum blonde.

Everyone went silent. I stared at her in disbelief. Ella smiled coyly back under the slick curtain of her hair. It was moments too late before I realised who she was flanked by. Jane Ayres stared at me with the triumph of a birthday girl who had received her best gift ever.

"Hi Lizzie," said Ella.

"Hi Ella," I said back. "Will you folks please excuse us? We have a few things to talk about."

I shot Jane Ayres a dazzling smile and grabbed Ella's arm, making sure I twisted it real hard. Then I dragged her off.

"Let go of me!" protested Ella.

"Scream and you'll cause a scene," I said through clenched teeth. "Is that the look you want to be debuting tonight?"

Ella shut up immediately. I pulled her into the dining room and slammed the doors shut.

"What the hell do you want from me, Eliza?"

I had underestimated Ellanoir Dashwood. I couldn't believe this was happening. Marianne had been right after all.

"Um, well — maybe to act like a friend?"

"I'm sorry?"

"You're not sorry, Ella," I said to her calmly. "You're just an ungrateful little skank. After I got sucked into being your friend and I introduced you to my nice friends, getting them all to accept you — this is how you repay me?"

"Hang on," said Ella, all of a sudden. "Introduced me to your *nice* friends? For your information, Eliza, don't you think I'm capable of making my own friends? And honey, you obviously don't hear much of your own publicity, 'cos from what I've heard — you aren't that *nice* a bunch of girls."

I lunged at Ella and I tried to grab her. And trust me, I didn't care what I grabbed; I just really, really wanted to hurt her. I swore if my fingers closed around her neck, I would have strangled her.

Ella screamed and scratched at me with her newly painted black fingernails, but I managed to take hold of her wrists.

"What did you do to get to Jane Ayres? And don't try to deny it. As if she would suddenly decide to be friends with someone like you! I saw you talking to her on Friday. Tell me what you did!"

"Okay, okay," yelped Ella. 'Let go of me first."

"You promise? Don't screw around with me!"

"Yes!"

I let go of Ella. I realised I'd gripped her so hard my own hands had turned red.

Ella brushed the hair off her face and adjusted the bottom of her tiny dress.

"I told her that it was us who attacked Neil's house, okay?"

"*What*? Okay, firstly, don't ever use the word *us* again. You are no longer part of *us* and secondly — do you know what will happen if she tells Hollerings we broke the curfew? They take the whole 'curfew' thing seriously, I mean, ever since Frank Bruno—"

"No, she won't," said Ella in a quiet voice. "She said she'd keep it to herself. She's not the monster you make her out to be. Have you ever considered that it might be you who are the monsters?"

Ella looked down at her wrists with the outlines of my fingers still on them. I didn't realise how hard I grabbed her. I covered my mouth with my hand.

"For your information, Jane was impressed that for once someone was honest with her and told her the real story behind the rubbish rumours that go around this school. Maybe she saw that as a great quality to have in a friend. It's not my fault she thinks I'm better than fat Jane Mutton. I reckon she thinks that I'm game, like you all are."

I stared at Ella. At her little black dress and her six inch black stilettos and her fake blonde hair.

"Ella," I said slowly. "For your information, I don't think Jane Ayres thinks that you're 'game' or have any redeeming qualities of a great friend. Jane Ayres is just impressed she now has a better spy and an even more desperate bitch to do her dirty work. So congratulations to her and good luck to you, 'cos you'll need it!"

I let myself out. Behind me Ella sulked down into one of the ugly gold dining chairs.

"Lizzie!" Lexi raced up to me with Marianne following behind. "What are you doing with Ella? And what did Ella do with her hair?"

"You have *no* idea. But first I've got to find Jane Mutton—"

"Well, hello ladies."

Daniel Smalls and Gauntly had arrived.

Marianne crossed her arms. Lexi crossed her arms. I crossed my arms.

Smalls was wearing a tartan shirt tucked into his pants. His stomach looked like a whale stuffed into a set of bagpipes. Gauntly was dressed like he was going to his own funeral.

"My, my, Jones, you look all right tonight," said Gauntly, eying Marianne. "Don't you look something fine, done all up like a Union Jack?"

"Shut up," replied Marianne, giving him a fierce look. "If I want fashion advice from someone who looks like they've just crawled out of a coffin, I'll ask. And I didn't."

"Ooooh!" Smalls snarled and he grinned at Gauntly. Gauntly grinned at Marianne.

"So, Jones, what do you drink?" he said.

"Cranberry and soda."

"Can I get you a drink then?"

"Yes," replied Marianne, rolling her eyes. "I am, like, so parched."

Gauntly stuck out his arm. Marianne wrapped her arm around it and they walked off.

"What the—?" I stared at Lexi. Lexi gave me a "don't ask me" look back.

"What are you staring at?" I shouted at Smalls. He quickly retreated.

"Unbelievable," I said. "Can things *get* any more weird?"

Lexi sneezed. "I don't feel so good."

I pressed my palm onto her forehead. It felt warm.

"Go get yourself something to drink," I told her.

I grabbed one of the Art girls that Lexi and Marianne had been talking to earlier.

"Hey, er, whatever your name is, can you take Lexi out to the kitchen and get her a drink? Thanks."

I watched her take Lexi away.

I shouldn't have let her go.

◆❖

"Marianne?"

I tapped her on the shoulder.

She was sitting outside on the porch steps with Gauntly, watching the fairy lights. *How romantic.* It took me a while to find where she had disappeared to in such a spectacular fashion. She appeared to be having a good time, but not only that, she was laughing and *leaning on Gauntly's arm.*

"Can I please talk to you?"

I picked her up by the arm before she had a chance to reply.

"What?" replied Marianne, after I had dragged both of us into a corner.

"What's up with *that*?" was all I could say.

"*Oh.* You mean Lincoln."

"Lin — *ugh*! Gross! You mean Gauntly!"

"Yes," said Marianne, looking impatient. "So what about it?"

"We hate Gauntly! What about the crap in English? What about all those times you complained about him being an ugly, skinny git?"

"No, hang on. You mean *you* hate Gauntly. I never said I did. And as for—"

Marianne stopped. She picked at a lock of her hair and twirled it with a smile on her face.

"Stop," I said. "Spare me the details."

"Lizzie — all I can say is that when boys pull girls' pigtails, it doesn't necessarily mean it's because they hate them."

"Gauntly is friends with Biggins and Smalls! What do you expect us to do, hang around in one big happy family? Haven't you even stopped once to think about me? Or is that too much to ask?"

"Cut it out," said Marianne. And she was serious. "This is a party; try to loosen up. It's one night, it doesn't mean anything."

She tried to get away from me then, but I kept her pinned in the corner. At that moment, I kind of hated her.

◆❖

When I think hard about it, I find that I…actually don't like many people. I must be such an angry person.

◆❖

"Oh, by the way I think you must have forgotten something." Marianne put a hand on her hip. "Gauntly is friends with Neil, too."

She pushed past me. I let her go. Neil? What did Neil have to do with any of this? We were supposed to be talking about *her*. I hated how she tried to turn this back onto…ugh. I hated how she always thought she was so smart. I hated how she was so smart.

I was thinking I should probably go and check on Lexi, or find Jane Mutton and have a conversation about what to do with a little problem called Ellanoir, but at that moment the Jane that I really didn't need came barrelling at me.

"Boans!"

Jane Ayres was dragging something along with her. A something that turned out to be Aardant. Jane pushed him in front of me. I gasped.

Aardant's nose was purple. It looked huge. I notice he had a bruised eye and busted lip as well. Behind him, Jane's face lit up with a look of satisfaction.

"I want you to explain this, Boans, as I have been unsuccessful in getting my boyfriend here to explain anything."

"I — I don't know anything."

I frowned and shifted my eyes sideways so I didn't have to look at him anymore. I couldn't help it. Aardant's injuries were freaking me out. It would have taken someone with a lot of strength to do something like that. Or someone with a lot of hate.

From the corners of my eyes I could see a small curious crowd build around us on the porch.

"Let's go," said Aardant. "You're embarrassing us. I told you, I was playing football—"

"Don't lie to me," said Jane, "Boans here is going to tell me what happened."

"Well, I'm sorry," I replied and I looked her in the eye. "If boyfriend won't tell you and you're reduced to intimidating an innocent person that you just happen to hold a grudge against. That says a lot about your relationship, doesn't it?"

I heard a few breaths being sucked in. Good. I ran

my eyes over the faces surrounding us and then turned back to Jane.

"You *scrag!*" exclaimed Jane. She looked as angry as hell. "Look at him! I know there's only one person capable of something like this. That would be your scummy-excuse-for-a-human boyfriend, Fernandes!"

I laughed. "Neil? Neil is not my boyfriend. And if *your* boyfriend is too scared to say anything, then it's really not my fault you're dating such a pussy—"

"That's it, Firecrotch!"

Jane pounced. I felt her take hold of my hair and pull hard. Pity. Marianne spent ages putting the curls in too. My arm thrashed around in the air until I felt the back of her neck. I dug my fingers in hard. I decided it was hard enough when I heard her scream.

I felt strong hands on my shoulders pulling me away. They didn't hurt me like I expected them to. They were gentle and familiar.

"Neil!" I shouted, turning around.

"C'mon, Eliza, you don't want to hurt her," said Neil.

"What happened to your face?"

There was a pink bruise across it shaped like a palm.

"Got slapped playing touch rugby with girls." Neil smiled and wiped his cheek.

The crowd around us had grown bigger. I could see people holding out their mobile phones. All of them just standing there, staring.

"Come with me,' said Neil and he held out his hand.

I looked at Jane, her hair blonde and her face red. Surrounded by all those people still filming. I turned back to Neil.

"That's right!" said Jane loudly. "Go with that psycho monster! If you're stupid enough to trust him!"

I looked at Neil. I wanted to say *thanks for helping me,* but instead I said:

"Is it true? Did you beat Aardant up?"

"Yes," he replied.

Behind me I could hear Jane Ayres triumphant snort.

I looked at the hand Neil still held out to me, so gentle, so familiar. The same hand that apparently could become a stranger's fist. I turned away from him and pushed past the crowd and back into the house.

The triumphant snort of Jane Ayres followed and wouldn't let me go.

◆❖

I found Lexi hanging out the back, where a huge TV screen the size of the wall was blaring out a noisy video clip.

"I don't feel very good," Lexi said and tried to put her arms around me. I pushed her gently away.

"Have you seen Jane Mutton? I need to talk to her — Lexi, what have you been drinking?"

I took the cup from her and sniffed it.

"Who gave you this?" I demanded.

"Oh, Ronnie did," replied Lexi and she rubbed her eyes. "You know, that girl you handed me to?"

Ronnie Wood was standing nearby, talking to some other random Art student.

"...the graffiti here is so boring. In Melbourne graffiti is, like, art. What do you think Erica? Is it, like, art or vandalism?"

I coughed through the weed smoke and fanned it away. *Bloody hell*, I thought. *My outfit is dry-clean only.*

"I thought I told you to get Lexi a drink?" I said to Ronnie and I held the plastic cup up to her face.

"I did," she replied.

"I meant, as in getting her some frickin' *water*. Can't you see she's sick?"

"What is your problem?"

"Nothing," I replied and I threw the alcohol, plastic cup and all, on her. "There you go. You figure out if that is art or vandalism. Jane!"

I grabbed a stumbling Lexi and ran after the bright pink bubble.

Jane Mutton stopped and looked at me.

"Lexi is...tired. Is there somewhere she can lie down for a bit?"

Jane stared at Lexi and then back at me.

"She can go upstairs to my bedroom."

"Thanks," I replied. "Lexi? Did you hear that? Go up to Jane's room and I'll come and see you in a little bit.

Me and Jane need to have *talk*."

Lexi nodded and untangled herself from me. Shakily, she headed for the staircase.

"Well," muttered Jane. "Congratulations on roughing up the birthday girl and almost destroying my party. By the way, you'll get your fifteen minutes of fame on the net tomorrow."

"Just cut the crap, Jane," I replied. "I didn't decide to stay to hear you have a go at me. I've thought about what you said before and you're right. We have to do something about this."

"Well, do you have a plan?"

"No," I replied. "I haven't had time to think. You might not believe it, but I actually have had a lot to deal with tonight already."

"And you think you're the only one?" Jane said mockingly, with a fake look of surprise. "Look at me. I planned this entire party just for Janey. I had to lie to my parents, who trust me, and I have spent God knows how many hours making frickin' rocket and goats cheese mini-pizzas, and has she even bothered to say thanks? If you're going to come up with something Boans, you better come up with it fast!"

"Jane Ayres is right behind you; just shut up and smile." I spun her around quickly.

The birthday girl, looking a little worse for wear, came marching toward us with Aardant in tow.

"Well, well — still here, huh?" She spat at me.

I stared at Aardant. Even though he was holding hands

with Jane he looked like he couldn't wait to get away. I almost felt sorry for him.

"That's right," I said loudly back. "I couldn't resist, er… Jane's beautiful mini-pizzas. Which she made *herself*."

Jane Mutton nodded and stared at Jane Ayres with big, hopeful eyes.

"Right…" said Jane and she frowned. "Whatever. But then I want to see you gone. This is my birthday and I am officially bouncing you out. And if I see your scummy boyfriend show his face here, I'll see to it he gets as good as he dishes out."

"Actually, this is Jane's party." I slapped my hands onto Jane Mutton's shoulders and plastered a wide smile across my face. "If Jane was my best friend, I would tell her exactly how grateful I was. Like, *now*."

"Jane. It was very nice of you to organise this party for me," replied Jane. "You didn't have to. In fact, I didn't ask you to. Please consider this the very last time that your name is attached to mine. After this party is finished, I want you to know that our friendship is as well."

A noise that sounded like Jane Mutton's little designer-dog made me block my ears. I realised the sound was coming from Jane Mutton herself.

"Why, Janey? After all these years, what have I done to make you hate me?"

Jane's expression said she couldn't be bothered explaining, but then a look passed over her face that said that the opportunity was too good.

"Jane…I don't know what to say, so I will try and be as nice as possible. You bore me. You're stupid and a horrible dresser. Did you think you were ever anywhere near my league, let alone in it?"

Jane Mutton's mouth popped like a goldfish. Jane Ayres turned around and reached out for her boyfriend's hand, but the other Jane was not ready to give up yet.

"Jaaaaney!" she wailed and she stumbled forward with her arms out.

Aardant put his arm protectively around his girlfriend and looked at Jane Mutton.

"Leave her alone — don't you understand anything, fatty?"

Jane Mutton might have stood for being called boring, stupid and a horrible dresser, but she wasn't going to stand being called fat. She heaved up her short frame and punched Aardant in the face.

There was a scream and Jane Ayres had Jane Mutton by the hair. Aardant was making groaning noises, his hand over his nose, blood trickling over his fingers. I made a mental note to shave my head next time I planned to get in the ring with Jane Ayres.

"How dare you!" Jane was screaming.

"I don't regret that one tiny bit!" Jane was screaming back. "I'm glad Neil kicked the crap out of him as well!"

It took me, hauling Jane Mutton backwards, and Marianne hauling Jane Ayres in the opposite direction, to break up the fight.

"Where have you been?" I asked Marianne. Her hair was all messed up.

"Nowhere," she snapped, too quickly. "I think I should ask you the same question."

"Nowhere myself." I stared at her, refusing to be the first to look away.

I let go of Jane Mutton. Across from me, Marianne dumped Jane Ayres from her arms as well. We all stared at Aardant. Blood was dripping off his chin and onto the tiles. Marianne stuck her hand down the front of her dress and extracted a linen hanky.

"Feel free to keep it," she said as Aardant looked at it suspiciously and then pressed it against his nostrils. Blood roses bloomed on the fabric.

"Alistair," said Jane Ayres, brushing hair from her face and stumbling in her high heels. "You are a disgusting mess. As if you didn't look bad enough already. Go clean yourself up."

"Yeah," chirped Jane Mutton. "Do as she says. 'Cos how can any other girl possibly be jealous of her when you look like that? In front of so many people."

I could see Aardant's fist clench itself into a ball. I put my hands on Jane Mutton's shoulders. As we're not friends, I'm not going to say "protectively".

Aardant was staring at Jane Mutton in such an intense way that I started to get scared. I mean, sure, the insults, scratching and the hair-pulling was not exactly earning anyone halos, but…

His eyes were the same as Neil's: dark in colour, but while Neil had the eyes of a languid baby deer, Aardant's looked like they belonged to the hunter on the other side of the gun.

I tightened my hand on Jane's shoulder.

"Let's just go now," said Aardant and he grabbed Jane Ayres' hand.

Jane drew her hand sharply away. "I would leave right now if I could. But this is *my* party."

She turned toward me and Jane Mutton.

"Since you've ruined my entrance, Boans, and you've ruined my boyfriend, Mutton, then I suggest you both stay out of the way and don't ruin the rest of the night for me."

She pushed past Marianne and stormed off alone.

Jane Mutton didn't reply. She glared at Aardant and pointed upstairs.

"Powder room up and to the right. Go clean yourself up, you pig."

She stomped off in her ex-friend's wake. Aardant followed, slowly steaming.

"Fun party, isn't it?" commented Marianne.

"Oh, I'll remember it for years to come," I replied.

"So what now?"

I looked at the hair all fluffed up at the back of her head.

"Maybe you should go back and continue what you were doing before," I said coldly. "I'm going to go upstairs too and check on Lexi. One of your friends got her drunk."

"I'll come with you," said Marianne undeterred.

She followed me through to the foyer and then stopped. She bent over and picked up something next to her feet. "But first, I think someone wants our attention."

She stretched her hand out toward me. Sitting in her palm was a rock. Another one came scuttling across the marble floor and bounced off my leg.

I looked out the open front door. The crowd that had gathered around so eagerly before had all dispersed to the back of the house to stare aimlessly at the TV and drink and smoke and hook up. There was only one person left. Neil.

I watched the smile spread across Marianne's face as she bent down and collected the other rock into her palm. I felt something burn inside me. I looked at Marianne, with her thin waist and her generous cleavage spilling over her dress and it burnt even more. It was possible I was jealous.

"Seeya," I found myself saying and I marched out the door. Even though I told myself that I never wanted to see him again. I just didn't want it to be Marianne instead.

"What?" I said to Neil when I got close enough. He was standing in the middle of the lawn, both hands shoved in his pockets. "You better have a bloody good reason to come back."

"Rat B died."

"Oh," I said. "I thought he was getting better."

"So did I."

"I...I'm sorry."

I truly was. I thought about Professor Adler then. I thought about him pressing that trigger in class, again and again. Then I thought of Neil and his fist coming down on Aardant, again and again.

Neil reached into his pocket. Rat B's eyes were wide open and beady. Looking at him, I was glad he had left his painful shell of a body.

"What are you going to do with him?"

"I reckon I'll bury him by the Linden tree. Next to the shrine for Tacky."

"Is that still there?" I asked, surprised.

"Why shouldn't it be? It's always been there," replied Neil and he looked at my face.

I have known Neil for so long he has almost become a second skin. I thought I would always be comforted knowing he was there. Like my favourite pair of old bed-socks.

Under the night, beneath the strings of white paper lanterns, Neil looked...different. I always knew we could be a lot of things to each other. I just never thought it would be...weird.

"Why did you have to do that to Aardant?"

Neil shrugged and looked down at Rat B.

"Maybe I'm just a psycho monster. You tell me," he said.

Maybe you're a dick for trying to be Marianne's knight in shining armour, I wanted to say, but instead I thought that earlier that evening, Ella had called *me* the monster.

"Why are you so angry all the time, Neil?" I said, irritated.

"If I'm the kettle then hold on a second there, pot," replied Neil and he put his hand out to touch me. I smacked it away.

"It was because of Marianne, wasn't it?" I wasn't prepared to let it go. I know I should have.

"I thought we are all friends."

"I wish we weren't."

"You don't mean that."

"Yes I do!" I was so annoyed. I took off my heels and threw them one by one toward the street. Then I paced up and down on the lawn in my bare feet.

"What is this about Marianne, anyway?"

"You tell me," I shot back using his words. "You spend four hours a week alone together. Aren't you, like, *soulmates*?"

"I don't know what you're thinking, but Marianne spends most of that time writing notes, asking questions and ignoring me. When we talk about Chemistry, there's more sparks flying between Mari and her textbook. Not Mari and me."

I picked at the flaking skin around my fingernail.

"What do you honestly think of her?"

"She's brilliant, of course."

"See?" I pointed out.

"Have you ever considered that it's not all about Marianne? Maybe sometimes it's about you."

I folded my arms and walked back up to him. We both stared down at Rat B in his palm. He looked so warm and furry, still.

"Anyway, I doubt I'm a bad enough boy for her. What do you think?"

I was thinking *Neil is a good guy. Neil's promises are good.* I searched accusingly for traces of regret in his voice. I came back empty.

"I remember when you used to come over," he said.

"It was my dad who used to bring me over."

Ouch. I didn't mean for it to come out that way. I didn't mean to say that I didn't like him...for the hundredth time, I should have apologised. Instead I shrugged. I didn't particularly want to talk about what had been and what could have been.

"My dad is long gone."

"Elle, have you ever wondered why your father used to bring you over all the time? When *my* father wasn't around?"

"They were friends," I said firmly. "They went to uni together. Just like Marianne and Lexi's parents are friends with your parents. Maybe they thought the idea of us playing together was cute, I don't know."

I ignored that he called me *Elle.* No one calls me that except him.

Neil smiled. It looked painful.

From somewhere inside the house drifted a tuneless *Happy Birthday*. Jane Ayres must be cutting her cake. Her three-storey cake, made to look like a white castle, with marzipan turrets and sugar flags. To house the precious princess inside of her.

"How long has it been? Ten years now? More than that? Look, I'm sorry that your superhero dad flew away. I wished he'd stayed if that meant I'd get to see you. I still miss that you never come around anymore, Elle. Even after all this time."

I forced myself to stare into his eyes. Brown. Belligerent. Bambi.

"Neil—"

"Elle," said Neil. "If you weren't grounded from going to the ball, I'd ask you."

Out of the blue, the sprinklers came on.

We stood for while, slowly soaking.

"I'd better get going," he said finally.

"I guess," I replied.

We had said too much. It wasn't good. But neither of us moved.

I watched the water drip off the end of his nose and onto his lips. He brushed his wet hair back. Neil looked so solemn. So pale. Quiet and handsome.

"Say hello to Tacky for me, won't you?"

Neil nodded and put Rat B back inside his waistcoat pocket. I watched him as he walked off down the driveway. Hunched over against the world in his black knee-length coat, he looked like a semi-colon.

◆❖

Back inside the house, someone pushed a plastic plate with a sliver of chocolate mud cake into my hands. I shovelled at it absentmindedly with my spork until it turned into mush.

I don't know why it took me so long to go and find Lexi. I guess things got in the way.

"Lexi? Are you in there Lexi?"

The plaque on the door, edged in fluffy pink marabou, read *Jane* in glitter lettering. This was definitely the right room.

"Lexi, please open up if you can hear me. I'm worried about you."

I knocked gently on the door.

"Lexi, can you hear me?"

"Go away!" came the muffled reply.

"Lex, this is Eliza. I'm not a Jane Blonde, if that's what you're worried about. Speaking of the Blondes, have I got a juicy bombshell for you. You're so totally going to love this. Turns out the rumours are true! It's all over!"

There was another muffled reply, but I couldn't make out the words. It was followed by a crash.

"Lexi, I'm going to come in, okay?" I put my hand on the door handle. "This is Eliza. Not a Jane Blonde. Not a stranger."

I pushed the door in gently. The room was black. The colour of Lexi's earrings, brushing against her neck like little black holes. I couldn't make out anything at first. I stood there and stared, waiting for my eyes to adjust to the dark.

The bed was empty. A little shockwave rippled through

me and I stopped breathing. Lexi was balled up in the corner, hiding behind a pillow. Next to her was a broken lamp.

"Lexi?" I said and I walked slowly toward her. I knelt down. "Babe, what are you doing on the floor? Come sit up on the bed with me."

Lexi shook her head. I leaned over and looked into her face. Lexi's eyes were wide. I couldn't see any visible tear tracks on her face. She looked a little pale, but that might have just been from the moonlight.

"Do you want to go home now? Tell you what, I'm kinda getting sick of this party myself. It really does suck big time. Worst. Party. Eva." I said and I laughed.

Lexi didn't laugh back. She didn't say anything. She just stared straight ahead, hugging the pillow in front of her.

"What's happening in here? Why are you both in the dark? Can I turn the light on?"

I heard the shuffling of Marianne's ridiculous dress and then felt the smoothness of her leg as it came to a stop against my arm.

"What's wrong with her?"

"I don't know. I bet it's got something to do with whatever drink your Art friends gave her," I said. "Ditzy scrags."

Marianne crouched down next to me.

"Lexi? Can you hear me?"

Lexi didn't respond. Marianne turned to me.

"Something is definitely wrong with her. Maybe she's drugged?"

"Well if she is, I can bet it's got something to do with your hippie friends—"

"Shut up," said Marianne. "That's not helping. Let's see if we can get her up. Here, you take one side and I'll take the other."

I took Lexi by the arm. As soon as we started to pull her upwards, she started to struggle. And boy, could she put up a fight.

"This is not helping either," I shot back at Marianne.

"Well, what do you propose we do? Come on. Just hold her tighter."

"Marianne! We can't do this. I have never seen Lexi like this before — something is wrong, Mari — stop! Just stop!"

I shouted so loudly I scared myself. Marianne jumped and dropped Lexi's arm.

"Okay, okay, just quit shouting at me!"

"Listen Marianne," I said slowly and firmly, "when I ask you to do something I want you to respect me. End of story. I am the boss, not you. If you want to throw a tantrum and walk now, go ahead. Go to Jane Ayres. I am sure she will ditch Ella and sign you up in a heartbeat 'cos we all know who her first preference has always been!"

Marianne looked hurt, but I didn't have time to care about her feelings. I put my hand on Lexi's face. She was trembling. Like a little animal.

"Lexi, do you hear me? You have to tell me what happened."

Lexi looked up at me and blinked.

"He came in here. I gave him a hug."

"Who? Who came in here?"

Lexi couldn't say the words. She opened her mouth, then she closed it again.

"I gave him a hug. All I did was give him a hug!"

It was then that I realised I was wrong in thinking that I knew who the monsters were. Maybe each of us, in turn, is a monster to someone else.

◆❖

"You have a blood nose," says Dr Fadden. He pulls a hanky from his pocket.

I touch my nostril. I recoil at the sight and close my hand over my nose. Great, I've moved beyond tears and now it's blood. I wonder if something is haemorrhaging inside my head.

Neil said that there's a time to keep it in and a time to let it out: if you let it sit too long inside, it'll turn into poison.

"*That* is my story," I spit out. My throat feels so dry. "Now you keep your side of the bargain. I want to see Lexi."

nine

I blamed Marianne's Art class friends for giving Lexi the drink, but the ugly truth was, it was me who had made the punch in the first place. One half Marianne's tin of fruit salad and one half Jane Mutton's bottle of vodka. We were all one part guilty, but none more so than me.

Lexi was prepared to talk only to me. *Alone.* I don't think Marianne will ever get over that.

She said that she started to feel funny as soon as she went off with Ronnie Wood. You know, during that grand moment when I sold her out. She held it inside because she wanted to be social and she was so scared that she would vomit on Ronnie.

After she went upstairs she fell asleep. She didn't know how long she'd been out until she heard water running on the other side of the wall. The water stopped and she heard someone come into the room.

Aardant had a ball of toilet paper pressed against his nose. Lexi sat up on the bed and Aardant asked if he could sit next to her. Lexi said he could. She heard the bedsprings creak under him because he was tall and muscular. And sexy, almost.

They talked for a little while. Lexi asked what happened to his nose and he asked her what was wrong with her. She said she thought she had the flu or something. She crossed her legs and tried to look pretty. Because you just never knew, maybe tonight some white-knight was going to dump his snotty girlfriend and throw you over his shoulder.

Lexi swore she didn't do anything after that. All she did was give him a hug.

Aardant stood up and undid his belt. Lexi tried to fight him off, but Aardant is a jock. Lexi does yoga, but she doesn't have the experience of knocking the crap out of a dozen other beefcakes on an oval. Afterwards he pulled his pants back up and left. Just like that.

◆❖

They've taken her to St Christina's Hospital. I'm glad. John Thompson was in a car accident once and he went to the public hospital in Middlemoore. He had to share a ward with a crazy old man who kept trying to get out of his own bed and into John's. They didn't believe him until the old man pulled his catheter out. There was a lot of blood on the linoleum floor. They believed him then.

Lexi has a room all to herself. It looks like a hotel room. There are so many flowers. That surprised me. I thought everyone had already dissed us; that they were just waiting for the news to tell them we'd been locked up for life. Then I remember it is not *us*. It's Lexi the flowers are for. They care about her. They never said anything about me.

"Go on," says Dr Fadden and he ushers me into the room. I see him nod to the nurse at the door. Then he steps back outside. The nurse looks at me full of suspicion. Maybe she's seen me on the news and is wondering where she recognises my face. Is it legal to put the faces of sixteen-year-olds on the TV and in the papers? I mean, aren't I a child that needs to be protected from predators?

I walk up to Lexi's hospital bed. She's hooked up to some sort of breathing machine that sounds like it's trying to suffocate her instead. There is a tube coming out of her arm that travels up to a bag of clear fluid. Her wrists are bandaged in white. She looks so terrible I have to look away.

What did I do to you? I want to scream. But I keep it on the inside.

Above Lexi's head hangs an icon of a saint. It must be Christina the Astonishing, the patron of this hospital. "Astonishing" because she died and then at her funeral, she woke and rose up to the rafters of the Church. Christina's mouth is grimacing, her eyes rolled upward. Her hands are tied together with rope, but she looks like she is praying. I look away. My hands are still bound with the metal cuffs. I feel broken and ashamed at the same time.

"It's my fault Lexi. Just look at you." I brush away a strand of hair on her forehead.

I wonder where Lexi is right now. Is she in a happier place? Maybe somewhere inside her head it is Saturday and she's shopping at that new bead shop on the Strip. Picking out crystals so she can make earrings to match her pink ball dress. Maybe she's floating somewhere on the ceiling right now. Looking down at her lifeless body and wondering whether to leave. I hope she sees me and knows I say *hold on*.

"Can I ask Marianne to come in now?" I asked Lexi.

She was still huddled in the corner of Jane Mutton's bedroom. She had been there all night. I had slept, or tried to sleep, beside her. Marianne, on the other hand, had spent the night pacing up and down the corridor until Jane told her to cut it out because she was wearing down their expensive carpet. When I went outside in the morning, Marianne squeezed the truth out of me.

Lexi nodded.

"Okay," she said.

Fury wrote itself like a scarlet humiliation on Marianne's face, among the smudged lipstick and mascara. She didn't want to look at me. She bowed her head and knelt down beside Lexi.

"We are going to do everything we can to help you, you hear that?" Marianne was speaking really slowly and loudly, as if Lexi's "accident" involved brain damage.

Lexi shook her head.

"What is there to help?" she replied. "It's already happened."

"Aardant's going to get his ass caned and then some. I'm going to make sure that he doesn't get away with this."

"How exactly are you going to do that?" asked Lexi. She bit the edge of her thumbnail. A piece of black polish peeled off.

Marianne was not prepared for the question. I wanted to blame Marianne for stuffing it all up at that moment. That would have made it easier.

Lexi watched her stumble on her words and I saw her trust in Marianne bellyflop too.

"We'll go to the police," blurted Marianne.

"No," said Lexi. "I want to go home."

Marianne lifted her eyes and met mine. This was the first that Lexi had said about wanting to move from her corner.

"We'll help lift you up," I said to Lexi.

"No," she replied. "I'm not an invalid, Eliza."

Marianne and I stepped aside. Slowly, Lexi pulled herself off the ground. She was as fragile as a newly hatched bird.

"Take me home," she ordered.

"Do you want to go to the bathroom and freshen up first?" asked Marianne. "Brush your hair, wash your face?"

"No, I don't want to *freshen up*. I just want to go home," replied Lexi angrily.

Marianne's face puffed up and she pulled me roughly to the side.

"We need to get her to the hospital or something," she whispered viciously into my ear. "So they can…do those tests and swabs and things. For proof. Like on *Forensic Crime Scenes* on TV…"

I looked over my shoulder at Lexi. She was standing with her arms wrapped around her body. In her jeans and her thin spaghetti-strap top. And here was Marianne talking about tests and swabs. I thought about how we couldn't move Lexi last night. How were we supposed to drag her to the hospital?

I imagined Lexi lying on a cold examining table being prodded and poked by some faceless doctor in a surgical mask. I looked at Lexi again. She suddenly appeared so small, so weak, and I knew I couldn't do it to her.

"Let her go," I said. "She just needs to have a shower, eat a decent meal and then maybe she'll be well enough to deal with this."

"No!" snapped Marianne. "She can't take a shower. That's going to wash away all the evidence, don't you watch *Forensic Crime Scenes*—"

"Marianne!" I butted in. "Do you remember what I said to you yesterday about where your place is? We're taking Lexi home. End of story."

Marianne looked at me like she had just swallowed a pill of contempt the size of a watermelon. Then without a word she turned and marched back to Lexi.

"Honey, we're going. Do you want me to organise someone to come and pick you up?"

"No," said Lexi. "I'm fine. I can walk. I *have* two legs."

I heard the sound of a car pulling up outside. Then of doors banging, a woman's voice shouting and a man's voice answering just as angrily back. Jane Mutton's parents were home from the counselling retreat. Must have gone real well by the sound of it.

"I need the lot of you to clear out right now." Jane stood in the doorway with an apron and rubber gloves on. "You're the last of the trash I need to take out."

"Thanks for letting us stay last night," I said and pursed my lips just in case I accidentally used the word "grateful".

"Make sure you use the back door and don't you dare let anyone see you," replied Jane coldly. She snapped a glove off and disappeared. But not before I caught what looked like concern tip the edges of her mouth.

Maybe we should have done what Marianne said. We could have convinced Lexi to go to the hospital and in some miraculous turn of events, she would have agreed it was for the best. Some really understanding Mary Sue doctor would do the rape kit, which would be analysed by some nerdy, heart-of-gold lab technician who'd match the DNA to Aardant. Then the cops, led by some really hunky detective, would go and kick down a door and nab Aardant just as he's about to commit the same act with another innocent victim.

Yeah, that might have been the story. Just like an episode of Marianne's favourite Thursday night cop show. If I hadn't made the decision to let Lexi go home and wash away the evidence, it could have been perfect.

Outside, Dr Fadden is leaning against the white corridor wall, talking to a young, attractive nurse. The nurse doodles something absentmindedly on her clipboard. Dr Fadden excuses himself when he sees me.

"Stop chatting up the nurses — you're not a real doctor you know."

I swear that for a second he looks hurt.

"Tired?" he asks.

I shake my head.

"Peckish?"

I shake my head again. But I realise I am. I didn't finish my double cheeseburger. It is a sick type of hunger.

Dr Fadden reaches into his coat and pulls out a plastic packet.

"I got this from the vending machine," he says and tears the top off. "While you were in there with Alexandria. How is she, by the way?"

"Asleep," I reply sarcastically.

"In case it interests you," he says, undaunted, "I served a stint in here years ago. All the patients used to walk the hallways in their pyjamas just like *One Flew Over the Cuckoo's Nest*. Considering the quality of the hospital food, I think the vending machine kept me alive. Here, hold out your hand."

I hold out both my hands. Not that I could choose. They *are* bloody chained together.

"Some for each hand. So that they don't fight. Like my mother used to say. Now let's go."

I have never heard anyone say that before. Maybe it's just Dr Fadden's mother. The fact that he even has a mother seems strange to me. He is so stiff and formal, I'd just assumed he'd exploded out of a rock one day as a fully-fledged bachelor.

I find myself standing there with both hands full of Skittles, trying to figure out how I'm supposed to eat them. It makes me smile. Oh well. We are in the mental ward after all. They have put Lexi, the most normal out of all of us, here. I wonder where that leaves me.

◆❖

We went to see Lexi after school on Monday.

"So how did it feel?" I asked her and I blushed because I knew I was asking the question wrong. *Again.* It felt like we were having a casual conversation about losing virginities. Oh God, maybe we were, but I never thought it would be like this.

"How did you feel?" I corrected myself. It didn't feel any less awkward.

Lexi didn't flinch. "I don't really remember," she replied. "You know, it's funny. After I knew what was going to happen, something inside of me just accepted it. I didn't even have to figure it out. It figured it out for me."

I nodded, but I didn't understand.

"You know what I thought about? I thought about how thankful I was to already have a dress for the ball. My beautiful pink half-dress made exclusively for me by Mrs Dashwood. Can you believe it? During a time like that. I thought about how I hadn't yet chosen my shoes and handbag, and that I should do that if I got out of this."

"Lexi," I said and I swallowed. "We're going to sort this whole thing out. We're going to take care of you. You will go to the ball and you will look beautiful. I promise."

"Will I?" replied Lexi. She looked down at her palms and then right through me. "Maybe the old me. Not this me. I don't think so. Listen to this, Lizzie — after I went home yesterday, I went to the fridge and I gorged myself on Black Forest cake. I felt so disgusted I threw the rest of the cake, box and all, into the bin. I tried to leave the kitchen, but I couldn't. I was still starving. So I ended up on the floor eating cake from the bin. Isn't that the most disgusting thing you've ever heard? My diet is ruined now. I won't look good in that dress, ever."

"Oh babe," I whispered and I wrapped my arms around her. She did not hold me back. It felt like she was made from the bones of a little bird.

◆❖

"What are we going to do?" I whispered to Marianne as we both stood cross-armed outside Lexi's bedroom door.

I could tell by the look on her face that Marianne was going to bring up that thing about the police and hospital again.

"We're not taking her to the police," I said before she had a chance to speak. "She's not well. She's telling me weird stuff — she said she ate cake out of a bin, for godsake."

I pressed my fist hard onto my heart as I spoke. Maybe I wish I could rip it out, so it would stop reminding me I was still alive. I could still feel his postcard there, and I ached.

"Then I don't know what to say," replied Marianne. "She doesn't even want to talk to me."

I could see the blue eyeliner from Saturday night still stuck in the corners of Marianne's eyes. Her white school blouse was creased and there was something that looked like a food stain on the front.

"No police. Right now she won't properly open up to me,

and like you said, she doesn't even want to talk to you! How is she going to say anything in front of a complete stranger?"

"I don't know," repeated Marianne.

"Mari — help me here!"

"No!" Marianne stopped and composed herself. "Well you didn't want my help Saturday, did you?"

"I am not asking you to help *me*," I replied. "Get over yourself Marianne! This is not a game — this is Lexi we're talking about! Tell me that you really care about her."

"Oh God," said Marianne. She wrapped her hands around her head and nursed it like I had cracked it open. "I don't know, I really don't. Why don't we go and talk to the student counsellor? She's an adult we can talk to, right?"

"Okay fine," I replied. "Let's do that tomorrow then."

"Tomorrow," Marianne repeated for no good reason.

"When will Lexi wake up?" I ask.

"She's being kept sedated for her own good," replies Dr Fadden. "They will bring her out of it tomorrow, with her father by her side so she won't go into shock."

"Can I be there?"

"Like I said, Eliza, I am under strict orders to keep all of you apart. If you wanted freedom, then you should have thought twice before breaking the law. This is not a game."

"I know this is not a game," I mutter. I sigh and I drop back onto the car seat.

"You should tell me what what's-her-name-bitch-face did to Lexi."

"*Doctor* Jennens did nothing to Alexandria. She is a professional counsellor and she has Alexandria's best interests at heart. What Lexi did was her action alone."

I stare at the roof of the car. The roof looks plush. I feel like I'm inside a velvet-lined coffin.

"I don't even know why I talk to you."

"Well, too bad, Eliza; you've already told me too much."

I can stop, you know, I think in my head. But I wonder whether that's true.

"Marianne and I went to talk to Miss Bailoutte." I pause to sulk. "Boy, aren't we glad we didn't tell her *everything*..."

"I've spoken to Miss Bailoutte. And you just didn't withhold information — you outright lied to her."

"What? Why would I lie to her? After all, it was Marianne and me who approached her. She didn't catch us doing something we shouldn't and beat a confession out of us."

"There you go. Let it all out Eliza. You'll feel better."

I don't know why, but sometimes it seems easier to talk while driving. Maybe instead of leather couches in psychiatrists' offices, patients should lie in the back seats of cars and be driven around and around, until all their stories have been told.

◆❖

I went to see Miss Bailoutte during recess on Tuesday. Dragging a half-dead Marianne behind me. Lexi was still at home. Her dad thought she'd caught a fever. In a way, she had.

Miss Bailoutte's quarters are on the other side of the lake adjoining the auditorium. The swallows were skimming the surface, leaving no ripples. The same swallows that Lexi said were bad luck. I blamed the swallows because I had to blame something.

We could see the library ahead. What used to be books and furniture were all charred and blackened inside the massive glass cylinder. It looked like a plastic pencil sharpener full of shavings. Any minute now, I expected a giant hand to reach down and empty it out.

Miss Bailoutte was drinking a cup of pale, milky-looking tea at her desk. She had wavy hair that's tipped blonde at the ends but brown on the top, suggesting that at some point she stopped bothering to colour her hair and gave up on her looks. She had a photo of her cat in an expensive frame on her desk.

"What can I do for you girls?" she said with a big smile.

When Miss Bailoutte smiles, she flashes all her giant horse teeth and foamy spit pools in the corners of her mouth. It didn't help that Miss Bailoutte liked to chew gum and talk at the same time.

"Is this about spare spots on the graduation committee? We still need lamington makers for the drive next week."

"Um…no. We've come to speak to you about Lexi Gutenberg," I said.

Beside me, Marianne looked haunted. She hadn't looked right since Saturday night. I wish she would just pull it together. After all, she wasn't the one going through this; Lexi was.

"Oh yes, Alexandria. A wonderful girl."

I wished Miss Bailoutte didn't have to try and sell Lexi to me.

"We want to tell someone something — in confidence. We thought we could speak to you."

"Yes?"

"It's about Aar— about Alistair Aardant. We were all at a par—"

I felt Marianne place her hand on my arm in warning.

Oh yeah. *The party.* No one was supposed to know about the party. If Miss Bailoutte found out about it and blabbed to Jane's parents, we'd all get into trouble. And no matter how much I didn't like Jane Mutton, it felt like we were all in this together now. We didn't have a choice.

"Alistair, he did…something to Lexi."

That was all I could say.

I was ashamed. I was ashamed for her.

I thought about what would happen to Lexi if the whole school found out. I mean, Lexi's father didn't know, and shouldn't he hear it first from her own mouth? I know I was making up excuses — but I couldn't do it. I couldn't confess what happened to Lexi. I couldn't say the *R* word.

Miss Bailoutte zeroed in on us immediately. She looked almost excited. It made me feel queasy.

"Alistair Aardant? The school football star?"

I should have known. But I said, "Yeah, that one."

I guess it is inconceivable that the school football star could rape someone. Maybe if we pointed our fingers at Gauntly, with the death metal in his ears, no one would be surprised. Maybe if it were Neil, the delinquent who beat up other kids for no good reason, they would have said they saw it coming.

"What did Alistair do?"

"He assaulted Lexi."

"In what way?"

"He tried to come onto her."

"And?"

"It scared the sh—, it scared the *bejesus* out of her. But it's all right — she managed to fight him off."

Marianne turned to me with her eyes wide. It must be how a rabbit caught in the headlights looks, shortly before it comes face to car tyre. But I couldn't help it. The way Miss Bailoutte was looking at me — she was almost salivating. I couldn't say it.

"Do you think Lexi did anything to encourage it?"

"No!" I shouted and tried to block the question. Easier than trying to block the doubts that I shouldn't have, but suddenly did have, ripping up inside my mind. Lexi said they "talked". What exactly did she say to him?

Oh God Lexi, are you telling me the truth? Oh God, why am I even...

"Come on now, girls, don't be afraid to express how you feel. I'm here for you to talk to."

I didn't want to express how I felt. I didn't want to talk about it. I just wanted something done about it.

"Maybe if you talk it through it will help you to better cope with the events, like where you were when the attack happened," suggested Miss Bailoutte with another smile.

I didn't like how Miss Bailoutte used the word *attack*. I thought about Lexi, sitting on Jane Mutton's bed next to Aardant, the boyfriend of one of the most popular girls at our school. Lexi wasn't walking down a dark alley; she didn't accept a lift off a stranger and end up in a ditch. She was right here, in East Rivermoor. With a friend of Neil's.

Last year, I went with my mother to some pretentious art exhibition with one of her clients — dark and tall, a human handbag. I only tagged along because my mother promised to buy me that new chocolate Cooper St dress. Anyway, there was one installation by this young guy who had made a model of a hotel the size of a dollhouse and wrapped in gauze.

I suppose I had a chat with him because he was the only decent person there. I was bored and my mum was more preoccupied with social networking. I guess I kinda thought he looked a bit like Neil as well.

He told me he was trying to highlight the suffering of those young women who had been murdered, trying to get the old cases re-opened. In between the layers of gauze he had inserted little pieces of glass, bottle tops and other pieces of refuse he had found at the bottom of that ditch. Apparently trying to "express the hidden pain" that society had long buried.

I asked him why he cared so much and he took out a photo from inside his jacket. It was a photo of one of the murdered girls, the first one. He said that although he never knew her, he couldn't put his finger on why it affected him so much; he felt it was wrong that those women could be thrown away like rubbish. He said he felt frustrated that no one seemed to care. At the same moment, we looked up at the crowd around us, all busy sipping their tall glasses of champagne, laughing and absorbed in one another, and we both knew that it was true.

◆❖

Miss Bailoutte stood up, teacup clunking, and waddled around to our side of the desk.

"I — I was busy," I stuttered. "It was Marianne who should have checked on Lexi. After all, it was her fault Lexi got sick in the first place. It was Marianne's idea that we go out past curfew that Thursday night in the rain!"

There, I said it. I was angry, I didn't care who heard. I didn't feel like holding back how I felt. Beside me, Marianne stirred. I turned to feel her backlash. Instead, what I was confronted with took me by surprise.

Marianne's eyes were huge and watery, like some Disney princess. Then she did something I have never seen her do in the thirteen years I have known her. She started crying.

"Oh no, my dear, you poor thing!"

Miss Bailoutte leaned over and hugged Marianne. Marianne didn't try to resist. In fact, looking at Marianne's face, it almost seemed like she was grateful.

"Um, Miss Bailoutte? We really have to go now. I just remembered we have to, um, help Professor Adler set up another one of his 'educational' experiments."

I tugged at Marianne's arm.

"Oh, of course," replied Miss Bailoutte absent-mindedly. "There, there dear. You know you can always come back at a better time, don't you? I will be here to talk."

I watched Marianne nod and wipe her eyes on the back of her hand.

"Let's go," I hissed into Marianne's ear and I steered her out by the elbow.

Outside, I confronted her.

"What was all that about?"

Marianne sniffed and hiccupped, but said nothing.

"Can't you see she's doing absolutely nothing to help us? Sitting around talking about how we feel and what it all means — what crap! Does it make a difference to Lexi? Marianne — *hello Marianne*! What is wrong with you?"

"Sorry if I happen to just appreciate a little bit of kindness! I'm human after all, Eliza. In case you forget!

Which is, like, something you do *all the time* these days."

I stared at Marianne, with huge tears dropping from her eyes.

"Marianne!" I shouted. "Sometimes I wonder why you are even part of our group. I mean, what makes you want to hang around with us when *everyone* knows you can do so much better with Jane Ayres?"

"Have you ever considered," replied Marianne, fully crying now, "that instead of trying to make myself look good — I might actually *like* you and Lexi? Is that too hard to believe?"

I never could have anticipated Marianne's response. I stood there speechless for a while.

"Let's just get to the next class," I said.

"What happened after that?" asks Dr Fadden.

"Miss Bailoutte took care of it all right. By the end of the day Aardant had been suspended. And the whole school knew about it. Because at about three o'clock the principal came on the intercom asking Aardant to come to his office."

"Isn't that good?"

"The whole school also found out why Aardant was suspended. I don't know which two-bit skank spread the rumour, but if I ever—" I stop myself. It is easy to let the blame tumble out of my mouth, like more dirty gossip. What was done was spread, but it was no rumour.

It was the words I had told Miss Bailoutte.

It was my *half truth*. My *dirty secret*.

◆❖

Lexi ended up being away from school for almost two weeks. Her father stopped believing she had a strain of the flu. He thought she was suffering from some other illness instead.

She told me how he had taken her to St Christina's to have her blood taken, three vials, exactly. How it was run through one-hundred-and-eighty-three tests, exactly. Lexi turned out to be perfectly healthy. The doctors didn't find anything except a mild intolerance to gluten. That was all.

◆❖

"I've got something to show you," says Dr Fadden.

He has stopped the car at a traffic light. The ticking indicator beats at the same time as my heart. The single red traffic beam fills up the car like an emergency light.

"Here," he says, popping his head up from the passenger side with a newspaper in his hand. He throws it over the backseat to me.

"What is it?"

"Check out the article on page three. There's a feature on your teacher, Miss Bailoutte. I thought you might like to know."

I unfold the paper. It's a copy of the *East Rivermoor Eye*. On page three is a picture of Miss Bailoutte. Her hair is freshly coloured and she is holding a framed plaque. The headline reads, "East Rivermoor Recipient of School Counsellor of the Year."

"No way," I say.

"Well, it's true."

"Do you know what?" I answer. "Neil told me once that I shouldn't worry about what happens to the people that do wrong, that there are forces in this world that will take care of them. You know what I think? That is just utter and complete crap!"

"Tell me more about Neil," Dr Fadden replies quickly, turning his head to look at me with one side of his face.

◆❖

I wanted to be alone. To stew over Miss Bailoutte. But there is nowhere to go in the new East Rivermoor. The park is purposely flat and bright green so that the fitness junkies and trendy young couples can be seen as they pose on the grass. Even the old peppermint trees that used to line the paths have been cut down, as if the whole goddamn suburb was scared of its own shadow.

I didn't want to go shopping, I didn't want to sit in a café and sip a mocha-soy-latte. I didn't want a pedicure or a manicure or my hair or my eyelashes curled. I didn't want something new. I wanted to be somewhere old. So I could contemplate, too, that I was slowly crumbling apart.

I was thinking all these things before I realised I had come to Captain Moore's House. I stared up at the red brick homestead of our founder, with its old-fashioned roses and wedding bushes studded with thousands of little white flowers. Still standing after all this time. The only old house left. I wonder what Captain Moore would think of this place today. Whether he would bother sailing all the way here for an exciting discovery-adventure if he knew it would one day be filled with pretentious townhouses and fashion boutiques.

In fact, the last time I had come here myself on a little curfew-breaking adventure of my own was…

"Looks different during the day, doesn't it?" The voice almost made me jump out of my skin.

Neil stared at me. I stared back at him. He widened his eyes at me mockingly.

"I've come here to pay my respects to your friends, the dearly departed." I put my palms out in front of me to show I meant no harm.

Neil smiled at me.

"Wow. Their first-ever visitor. Don't excite them too much now. I don't quite know how to crowd control a pack of itty-bitty rat zombies."

He swung himself past me. I scrunched up my face and held my breath. When I realised he hadn't accidentally brushed past me but was off out in front, I breathed out and ran to catch up with him.

At the bottom of the garden, under the big Linden tree, stood the tiniest tombstone you've ever seen.

"I got that in Dallas. I have to go back and get another for Rat B. You can get everything in America."

"Everything?"

"I stand corrected. Almost everything."

I turned my head and his face was right there over my shoulder. He smelt like something from a long time ago. Like butcher's paper, clag, cherry cough-syrup. The powdery scent of a My Little Pony.

"Um. So how was the Assassination Museum?" I asked, keeping perfectly still.

"The *Sixth Floor* Museum."

"Whatever. Do they display the gun that killed JFK?"

"No. I think it's still with the police, but I did look out the window where Lee Harvey Oswald stood when he shot the president. It was wicked," replied Neil. "I got myself a souvenir. You'll like this."

He reached down for his school bag and grabbed something out of it.

"Shit!"

"Here. Hold it."

"Are you sure?"

"Don't worry. It doesn't actually work."

I cradled the revolver in my hand. It was heavier than I expected.

I had so many questions. Why does Neil have a gun?

How did he manage to get it through customs without ending up on an episode of *Border Patrol*?

"I'm trying to fix it though. It's a vintage Colt Cobra, the same type that Jack Ruby used to kill Oswald."

I gave the gun back to Neil. I felt disappointed afterwards, my hand unnaturally light. Unnaturally empty.

"So when are you going back to America?"

"After the exams are over. New York. I'm going to Central Park to find Strawberry Fields."

"The memorial to John Lennon! I've heard the easiest way to find it is to look for the Dakota Apartments first, you know where he was shot, and then look across toward the park…"

If I wasn't mistaken, Neil was looking at me with the same expression I get when I am half-sick with nostalgia and summer longing.

"I was thinking maybe I'd go without my parents."

For a split second I had an image in my head of me and Neil walking under canopy of sunlight, staring at a mosaic with the word *Imagine* printed in the middle. I am eating a giant pretzel. Then I snapped back into reality when I realised I was dreaming. In so many ways.

"What you need to do is locate West 72nd Street — you're familiar with the grid system, I assume, since you've been to the US before?" I said hurriedly. "And where that intersects with Central Park West…will you send me a postcard, if I say please?"

"You infuriate me, Elle," replied Neil. 'But you wouldn't be so special if you weren't so awkward to deal with, huh?"

"The answer is no," I say to Dr Fadden. "Traffic light is green again. Keep your eye on the road."

That is the end of the conversation. I will talk no more. Not about Neil. Not to him. Not to anyone. We ride in silence all the way back.

ten

The day that Lexi came back to school, the only person who cared was me. She arrived in her father's sleek silver Lexus. I was prepared to be shocked. I had not seen her since he took her away.

Her father had decided that since nobody here could tell him what was wrong with his daughter, he would take her to a specialist in Sydney. Lexi and I spoke on the phone every night. She told me about the diet and the herbal remedies she was on. She was fine, only tired.

"I'm totally dying for a cheeseburger and fries," she said to me, and we both laughed even though it wasn't funny.

I had thought to myself that if she looked really pale or skinny I would be prepared for it. After all, she's had a rough couple of weeks. I thought I should stand close to the car in case she needed to be helped out, and if she hobbled I could help support her.

What I was not prepared for was for her to look absolutely normal.

To me it felt like the world had dealt Lexi the cruellest blow. It was like she had a giant wound inside of her, still fresh and bleeding, but which only I could see. She had no plaster casts, stitches or bruises to show for it.

"Hi," said Lexi.

"Hi," I said back.

"Where's Marianne?"

"She's at a Ball Committee meeting. The Aztec theme fell through because instead of giant Mesoamerican death masks, Caroline Aherne ordered giant Easter Island heads, which kinda screwed things up a bit." I replied weakly.

"She's busy, I get that," said Lexi.

We both stared at the school gates with our school motto wrapped around them like a ribbon: *Animadverto Vestri. Remuneror Vestri. Vindico Vestri.* Through it we could see a figure in the distance headed determinedly towards us. The Queen Bee — or should that be Queen Bitch — of the rumour mill, Kerry Croft.

"Hi, Kerry," I said.

She ignored me and turned to Lexi instead.

"So. Is it true that Alistair tried to come onto you?"

She made it sound like Lexi and Aardant were in the back row of the cinema and Aardant sprung a sneaky arm-over-the-back-of-the-seat on her.

"What's it to you?" I demanded.

Lexi touched me gently and turned to Kerry.

"Yes, Alistair tried to 'come onto me'. It was unwanted, if that's what you're trying to find out."

Kerry said nothing more. She just turned and walked back toward the school.

"Lizzie," whispered Lexi.

I took her small cold fingers and entwined them into my own.

"Go ahead then, Croft — go and spread that one around, you skank!" I shouted after her.

"How come Kerry knows?" asked Lexi.

I bit my lip. I hadn't told her about Miss Bailoutte.

"I don't know. I promise I never told anyone else. Why would I, Lexi? You don't think—?"

"No," said Lexi softly. "Of course not. I trust you."

I gave her hand a little squeeze. I hoped she couldn't feel my guilt.

◆❖

Marianne was already in the English classroom when we got there. And boy, did she look a wreck. Her hair was pulled back with what looked like a rubber band. There were several unidentifiable stains on her white blouse. The Marianne at Jane's party — the one in the neon purple heels and the wild dress, like a flag that mesmerised the red bull in Gauntly — she seemed like a dream now.

"Hi, Lex," Marianne said. She had barely wrapped her arms around Lexi before she sat down again to continue poring over her overstuffed folder.

"I just can't believe that Caroline…and even daring to cry as well when I kicked her ass off the committee! The new theme is Wild, Wild Western Australia — and this time I'm going to put myself in charge of ordering the nine-metre plastic Boab tree, in case I, like, end up with a one-foot miniature Japanese bonsai…"

Professor McFarlane, Marianne's Chem teacher, whom Mr Steele said had suffered a mild case of smoke inhalation during the library fire, died last week. While Principal Hollerings searched for a replacement, Marianne and Neil had their English lessons shifted to this class.

Marianne wanted to sit in the same spot she always sat in during her English class — i.e., my spot. On any other day, I wouldn't have let Marianne win. But because we found out Professor McFarlane died on the same day she broke down in front of Miss Bailoutte, I let her have her way. I sat on the other side of Lexi so I didn't have to be close to Marianne.

We heard male voices approaching the door, and I could feel Lexi tensing up next to me. Gauntly and Neil walked into the room. Lexi's body relaxed. I saw Gauntly give Marianne a long, brooding look as he followed Neil to the back of the class. Marianne didn't even look up from her folder.

"Wow, I see you're giving lover-boy your full attention," I said.

"Do I look like I have the time?" replied Marianne, my sarcasm going completely over her head.

Aardant stood in the doorway. I was the first to see him. I think his nose had healed, but now seemed to be slightly crooked. Lexi was distracted by Marianne selfishly sucking up all the desk space she could get.

I saw Aardant look directly at us. His eyes bore down on Lexi as she whined at Marianne and tried to push her stuff back onto her own desk. Something caught his attention and his eyes flickered to the back of the class. The smile from his face disappeared. I watched as he marched past us, his eyes returning to Lexi. This was when she noticed him.

I could feel her body tremble as their eyes met. Then he was out of sight. *Don't look behind you*, I prayed in my head. Other students started filing in then, thick and fast, and I was glad we were not so alone, so exposed.

Mr Steele made his flamboyant entrance about five minutes later.

"Okay, class. No more fooling around in the back seat of the panel van. We've come to the pointy end of the school year now. The outcome of this will separate the A-pluses from the A's for *Average* and the A-minuses from the B-pluses and the B-b-b-can do *better*. Can I please have your final assignments. Right. About. *Now*."

He marched up to the back of the class to start his collection. Usually, I would have turned around to smirk at the poor suckers who had forgotten, but now that didn't seem like such a funny thing to do. I didn't dare turn around.

"Assignments please, my ladies."

Mr Steele's hand was suddenly in front of us.

I slid my assignment out of its plastic sleeve and slapped it onto his hand.

"Thank you, Miss Boans. Miss Gutenberg?"

Lexi stretched her hand out with the paper and Mr Steele whipped it off her. "Thank you, Miss Gutenberg. I am impressed you had the time during your therapeutic sojourn. Do you feel better? *Good*. Miss Jones?"

It was then that I noticed that Marianne looked worse than ever. She stared at Mr Steele and turned a ghastly shade of white.

"I — I have it at home. It's on my computer. I just got confused because I don't usually have English class today—"

"No excuses please, Miss Jones. I expect more than that, especially from you. *My top student*."

I flinched. The remark hit me in the face like mud.

"Maybe I have a draft version somewhere in my file," said Marianne miserably.

Mr Steele stood patiently as Marianne took out another fat folder from her bag and started rummaging through it.

Under the desk, on my knees, I was balancing another crisp, neatly typed and stapled assignment. I had written up a completely different one as a backup for Lexi. Turned out I shouldn't have worried about her. I should have been worried about Marianne.

I slid the assignment onto Lexi's knee. She turned around to question me and I shifted my eyes toward Marianne, and then back at her. Lexi gave a little nod.

"Here Marianne, let me help you find it," said Lexi and she took the folder gently off Marianne. Then she dropped it. The overfull folder hit the floor and exploded.

"Oh! Sorry!" Lexi bent over to help gather the scattered contents. Marianne stared at the mess in horror.

"Oh, here Mari, I found it."

Lexi held my assignment up to her. Marianne snatched it from her and looked down at the cover page. Silently she held it toward Mr Steele.

"Thank you," replied Mr Steele coolly. "And for the entertaining little melodrama too."

He stared at the cover.

We all held our breath.

"Your name is not on this assignment," said Mr Steele after what seemed like an eternity. He handed it back to her.

"Sorry, sir," replied Marianne and she looked down. "I told you it was just a draft."

She hastily scribbled her name on the top. Mr Steele collected it back and shuffled it into the rest of the pile. Marianne's gaze temporarily brushed mine and I winked at her. It was my way of saying I forgave her for everything.

"Thank you people. Now, if I can get you all to take out your study guides. If you thought the mocks were hard, then you haven't seen anything yet. I will caution anyone in this class who isn't taking this 110 per cent seriously at this point to gather their meagre belongings and leave this room immediately!"

◆❖

Marianne approached me after class.

"Thanks," she said, bowing her head.

"That's okay," I said. "You are the top English student. You should try and keep it that way."

I know I should have been happy to see Marianne finally acknowledge her place, but I wasn't. I couldn't believe that the proud Marianne that I used to know, the one who, a month ago, would have torn up that assignment rather than accept it, now appreciated my small charity. I looked into her watery eyes and I felt…mean.

"Dux presentation in less than two weeks," I replied, trying to keep my voice strong. "You deserve to get the one for English, if not the all-rounder. So, congratulations."

"Lexi!" I called as she headed out of the classroom.

"Do you want to walk together to your next class?"

"Our classes are in the opposite direction."

"I know, but I thought—"

"I'm fine," she insisted. "Now I gotta go. See you at lunchtime."

I watched as she marched off alone.

"I won't be able to join you both for lunch. I've got a Ball Committee meeting," said Marianne, wiping her eye. "Hope you don't mind."

"I thought you had a meeting this morning?"

"Well, the ball's not going to organise itself," she snapped with the little energy she could muster. "I am the president. And I say that this *will* be the best ball ever. That is fact, not an opinion. As it is I'm missing a meeting because of my piano lessons."

"Why are you still doing piano practice? Can't your parents lay off you until after the TEE exams?"

"This has got nothing to do with my parents. I am fine. Now let's go."

On the other side of the corridor I could see Aardant, standing and watching the other students. His gaze shifted to us. Marianne took one look at him, flipped him the finger and kept on walking.

"What was that? You know better than to do something like that!" I grabbed Marianne by the arm.

"Of course I know better. It doesn't mean I'm going to behave better."

Marianne turned to me with a smile.

Now, *that was more like it*. I couldn't help but smile back. Then we both laughed. There she was, the old Marianne. Thank God for that.

"Oh hi. There you are. I've been trying to find you two."

Jane Mutton at three o'clock, heading straight for us.

Don't get me wrong. It's not like we were suddenly in club Share and Care. We still didn't like Jane and I don't think Jane liked us that much either.

"Frenemies?" I suggested. We shook hands. It was like we owed each other something now.

"How's it been?" I asked Jane.

"Complete bliss if I just ignore the taunts of being called Jane Nuthin'," she replied, friendliness toward me still foreign in her mouth.

As the three of us walked up the North Wing corridor, approaching from the opposite direction came two bobbing blonde heads. The timing couldn't have been any more perfect.

Jane and Ella. Now known as *Jella*. Or *Bonjela*, like the mouth ulcer cream. Which was appropriate 'cos just the thought of the two of them made my mouth flare up. They were inseparable now.

"Oh great." I put a hand as a warning on Jane Mutton's shoulder.

"What are we staring at then, Eliza?" said Ella.

What do you think I'm staring at? I thought, but was far too irritated by her trying to patronise me.

"If I remember correctly you once told me — after you got us both into trouble by running out of History — that I could pick who I wanted to be friends with. You promised you wouldn't even look in my direction?" Ella glanced at Jane Ayres as she said this. "So turn away then, Eliza."

I was fuming, but I couldn't think of anything smart to say because me getting suspended from that class and canteen duty wasn't funny. Apparently today, Ella was going to be witty enough for the both of us.

"Why don't we pretend that none of this ever happened and start from the beginning?" echoed Ella with more of my own words.

I pushed Jane Mutton and Marianne and we started walking.

"I hear that Lexi is back," Jane Ayres called over her shoulder. "I'm gonna get that little slut for what she did with my boyfriend."

"I'm not surprised she pulled that stunt. I always knew Lexi had validation issues," said Ella and she cocked her head. "She *is* a little fat."

Before I could react, the both of them were swept up and disappeared in the sea of students. Marianne looked at me with her mouth open.

"Bitch," I said under my breath to no avail.

We are back at the station. Dr Fadden unlocks the cuffs. I rub my wrists. They are painful and raw where the metal has cut into my flesh.

It's me who leads the doctor back to the interview room. I say nothing and neither does he; I know how this goes. I can fight it, but if I do then there will be more pain for me. I think of Rat B's broken body, and wonder if Neil had time to finish the shrine…

Dr Fadden sets up a tape recorder between us on the desk. One that actually takes a cassette tape. What the hell. Was he going to bring out a gramophone or Morse code machine too?

"What's that?"

"I'm going to record our next few conversations."

"I want to talk to you. I don't want to talk to a tape recorder."

"Just pretend it isn't there."

"You'll play the tape to other people. *No.*"

"Eliza," says Dr Fadden firmly. "I want you to tell me the truth now."

"You think I have been lying to you all this time?"

"You know what I mean," says Dr Fadden.

"No," I say, and fold my arms.

Does he think that because he's let me treat him like my own personal bitch that I now owe him? That he can just reach out and take what he wants; like Aardant thought he could take what he wanted? The thoughts in my head scream

I am not the victim. Lexi is the victim and no one helped her. I am not a victim victim VINDICTIVE—

"Do you even know what day it is?" asks Dr Fadden.

I refuse to answer.

Dr Fadden throws a paper down on the desk in front of me. It is another copy of the *East Rivermoor Eye*.

"This is the latest edition. Go ahead, turn to the social pages."

I look at Dr Fadden. His face says he means business. I take the paper and open it up.

"Your end-of-school ball was last night. Did you even know?"

I am crushed. The way he said it was so casual.

There is a four-page colour spread in the middle. I don't think I can look at it. There are too many faces I don't want to see, and too many faces I want to see but know won't be there.

"Look," says Dr Fadden and he points to the picture right in the middle so hard that his finger almost goes through the thin paper. "I believe this is the Belle of the Ball."

I want to throw up. I make myself look at the photo of Jane Ayres. I regret it as soon as I do. Suddenly something is howling inside of me. Howling to get out and I know it can't, because I have to keep it in.

"That's my dress," I say numbly.

My blue dress. The colour of a perfect blue sky. So perfect that there are no clouds. No clouds to rain on me. The dress

I wore when I stared up at Neil and he stared back down at me. He said I looked pretty strange, but in a good way. I had shed that dress onto Ellanoir's bedroom carpet and then for the rest of the night, I glowed in my own skin.

Ellanoir gave the bitch my dress.

"I can't deal with this," I say and I crush up the newspaper and push it back to him.

So it comes down to this moment. I either open my mouth now and say what I have to, or keep it inside of me for the rest of my life.

He is so close. He knows he is almost under my skin. He just needs something to tip me that bit sideways. I am like his little piggy bank with the coins finally rolling out. He has worked so hard. Trying to be my friend, trying to bribe me. I should have known better than to trust anyone. Maybe I have realised too late, again.

Dr Fadden clicks on the tape recorder. "Tell me about Neil."

"No!"

"Eliza—"

"Neil has nothing to do with it!"

"You tell me who does then."

It was Monday and I was staying behind after History to staple trial exam papers in Mr Gubler's classroom. I was grovelling big time because it looked like I was going to fail the History exam miserably, since Mr Gubler hadn't actually taught us, like, *anything* all term.

I stayed a little too late. When I lifted my head, Aardant was standing in the doorway. It looked to me like he had used his suspension to work on the highlights in his hair.

This is not good, I remembered thinking to myself. But at least I had the privilege of knowing. Lexi got no warning.

Aardant walked up to me. I took a step back. That was probably my mistake. He knew then that I was afraid of him.

"Oh, there you are, little snitch."

I held the stapler out. "Don't come any closer."

"What? Or else you're going to staple a study guide to my forehead?"

Aardant walked up to me and yanked a strand of hair out of my head.

"*Oww!*"

"Nice. If you like that colour. Although I'm kinda scared the colour's like that below."

How would he *eww eww eww*.

"But you're almost as pretty as Sexy Lexi."

I was still holding the stapler, but my hand was shaking so much I couldn't have pounded him in the face with it even if I wanted to.

"But not as pretty as Marianne. Now she's a lively one. Problem is, which one of you do I choose first?"

◆❖

"No more games, Eliza. I want you to tell me the truth now."

"I don't want to."

But I do. I know I do. I want to get rid of it.

"Then it will go back on Neil. He will carry the sole blame. That'll be easy, but I thought you said he was your friend?"

Very clever, Brian. I thought it would come to something a little more highbrow, but hey, it turns out to be blackmail. It'll get you anywhere, anytime. Congratulations, Brian.

"I'm listening," he says. I expect him to look all gloaty, but he doesn't.

I look over at the tape recorder. Then I reach out and turn it off.

"Then we do it my way."

◆❖

I ran straight to Politics the next morning, hoping to get there before Marianne. My mother had left another twenty-dollar note in the fridge, but I didn't take it. I knew I would get hungry, but I didn't want to eat. I wanted to know what it was like to be empty.

This was the first class since Lexi got back with all three of us in it. With Aardant. And without Neil.

I found Marianne walking by herself in the corridor. Blonde hair and long legs like a gazelle. I looked desperately around, as if I expected to see a hunter aiming a rifle at her.

I wanted to protect her. The best way I felt I could was to run up and hug her.

"What's wrong with you?" She pushed me away.

"Nothing," I mouthed, but the words didn't come out.

Marianne rubbed her right hand and I caught a wince passing across her face. She caught me staring and she dropped her hand.

'What's wrong?" I asked. I stared down at the hand and she drew it sharply behind her back.

"Nothing."

I didn't take that as a satisfactory answer. I grabbed her arm and held it up between us. Marianne looked away.

"Who did this to you?"

Marianne's hand bore the red marks where someone, very strong and very angry, had crushed it.

"He...he did," she said finally. I could see her trying to force herself to say his name. She couldn't. "He caught me when I was alone after I came out of the girl's bathroom. He must have been following me..."

"Did anyone see it?"

"What do you reckon? I think the answer to your question is *no*. I bet I could ask every one of those people who were there if they saw anything and they would say no."

"Why would Aardant do this?" I demanded.

Marianne looked down at the ground.

"He wasn't happy with...you know, after English yesterday? He said next time I did something like that again he would break my finger."

"Aardant is not a law!"

Marianne laughed.

"Yes he is," she replied and looked me straight in the eye. "*See Yourself. Reward Yourself. Punish Yourself.* You wonder why he got a one-week suspension? Because he thought that was all he deserved. And they agreed with him."

I grabbed Marianne's other hand and tugged her toward the classroom. Lexi was already there, sitting in our spot, waiting for us. I watched her chest heave as she spotted us.

"Have you gone through the latest test exam? I completed all the questions except for the last essay, I have no idea how to even start answering it — do you mind if I—"

"It's okay, Lex," I said. "We're here now. It's okay."

Lexi quit talking and tears pooled in her eyes.

I looked out the window. On the lawn, sprawled under the old ghost-gum beside the school lake, Neil was reading a thick textbook. I watched as he tossed it aside and took out a comic instead. I rolled my eyes and couldn't help but smile. I turned back to the classroom and stopped smiling. Daniel Smalls, Jeremy Biggins and Aardant walked in. Luckily, Mr Chifley was following directly behind them.

"Please take out the trial exam papers. I am allowing this period to be an open lesson. I know most of you will be spending the entire session slouching, gossiping and wasting my time, but even if none of you care about Politics, you might just care if you *fail*."

He's such a Mr Meanie. I so hated this class. I took out my file and looked over toward Lexi, trying to see the question that was bugging her. I could feel the breeze and the ruffling of my papers as Aardant walked past me to the front of the room. Lexi quivered.

I watched as he bent over in front of Mr Chifley so that our Politics teacher was completely blocked from our view. I shook my head and leaned back toward Lexi.

I heard the giggles from the back of the classroom when they first started, but I ignored them. It was probably Kerry Croft and her fangirls, making fun of the back of people's heads or giggling about some boy.

The giggles didn't go away. If anything they seemed to get closer until someone sitting directly behind me sniggered. I looked toward the front of the class. Aardant had said something to make Mr Chifley get on his high horse. I was thinking that Mr Chifley should probably be asking the class to tone it down, but then I realised that our Politics teacher probably couldn't hear anything over his own pompous voice. I felt a tap on my shoulder.

Cathy-Ann Moss was sitting behind me. She held a folded piece of paper toward me with a big smile on her face. I stared at her face long and hard. I should have known better than to accept another note from her. I didn't see the eager look in her eye. I didn't know that what she was handing me was bait.

Marianne and I had talked to Miss Bailoutte. Miss Bailoutte had talked to Principal Hollerings. Aardant had got suspended, had signed off agreeing that his suspension was what he deserved. It wasn't the outcome I wanted, but it was the best I could do for Lexi. I was past it. Lexi wanted to be past it. It should have been *over*.

I unfolded the paper. I folded it back up again and scrunched it in my fist, but it was too late.

"What's that?" asked Lexi.

"Nothing," I replied and I tried to catch Marianne's attention on the other side of Lexi.

Lexi caught that as well.

"Hand me the note," she said.

"No."

The same word a girl would say when there's a guy standing above her with his pants undone. The word wouldn't work this time either.

"If everyone else has read it and thinks it's funny then I want to see it as well. Hand it over."

I thought about Lexi sitting on Jane's bed. What did Aardant say to her when she said no? What about the girl whose lifeless body was rolled down into that ditch. How many times did she say "no" as she pleaded for her life?

Lexi snatched the note from me. Marianne sat stiffly on the other side, not knowing what to do.

There was nothing to read on that note. It was only a crude boy's drawing that didn't even look like the people it was supposed to show. That's why the arrow pointing to one of the figures was labelled *Lexi* and the other *Alistair*. Marianne peered over at the drawing and turned away.

Lexi's hand started to shake. Then she squashed the note back into a ball.

"Thi — this is not funny," she stuttered.

She stood up and she turned around to face the class behind her. The students in front caught on quickly and turned their heads eagerly.

"Who drew this?" she demanded. "You fucking show yourself to me!"

There was an audible intake of breath. Then everyone went quiet. When Lexi repeated herself, this time louder, no one dared to make a sound. Except Jeremy Biggins. Biggins looked straight at Lexi and sniggered.

I couldn't stand it. Sorry, but I *couldn't*. I was looking at Jeremy Biggins, staring at us with that snarling face and his ugly, crooked teeth. I could hear Mr Chifley still arguing some point a dead politician had once made and that no longer mattered to anyone, Aardant purposely egging him on so that our Politics teacher had no idea what was happening behind his back.

My father once told me that the hardest thing in this world was learning to say "no". Well, stuff him. He didn't know how to say "no", did he, when my mother forced him out of my life?

I got Mr Chifley's attention when I walked to the back of the class and punched that little runt Jeremy Biggins in the face. It was only when Mr Chifley heard Biggins' screams that he stood up and pushed Aardant aside. By the time he made it to the back of the classroom, Biggins was already writhing on the ground, dripping blood all over the new cream-coloured wool carpet the school paid a fortune for. What a shame.

I stood back and observed my work like I was an artist and Jeremy Biggins was my masterpiece. I've learnt a thing or two from Neil. And my new friend, Jane Mutton. Maybe I learnt a little something from Aardant as well — certain things aren't effective, but then, certain things are.

Biggins' blood was all over my hands. I turned to my right and through the window I could see Neil still sitting under the ghost-gum.

Neil look at me Neil look at me Neil look at me I repeated over and over in my head as I stared at him.

Maybe it's because we'd known each other before we were born. When our pregnant mothers used to sit with their swollen bellies facing each other, maybe we talked to each other as well and didn't need words. Otherwise, I didn't have any other explanation.

Neil suddenly lifted his head and looked straight at me. I walked up to the window, raised my palm and pressed it against the pane. It left a bloodied handprint. Through the red shape — my red flag, my riot sign — I could see Neil staring at me.

"Go get the nurse," Mr Chifley shouted at one of the other students.

Someone raced off and Mr Chifley turned his attention to me.

"You! Principal's office. Now!"

"Sir, I'm going as well. I was in on it."

It was Marianne. With her head bowed, she came to stand next to me.

"And me too."

I squeezed Lexi's hand as she joined my side and I looked Mr Chifley in the eye. On my other side I squeezed Marianne's hand.

"I don't know why I'm even doing Politics," I said to Mr Chifley. "I know all there is to know about democracy. I've voted on *Australian Idol* every season."

That definitely earned me that one-way trip to the Principal.

◆❖

"I — I don't want anyone else to see it," Lexi said as the three of us walked the cold hall toward Hollerings' office. "I feel so…ashamed."

I thought about the drawing. The only defence I had for my actions.

"Don't worry," I replied. "No one is going to see it."

"Does everyone think it was my fault?"

I bit the inside of my cheek. I could taste blood.

I'd faltered once. I doubted her; I failed her. The fury welled up inside me. It wasn't going to happen again, God help me.

"Lizzie?"

"Yeah?"

"Thank you for not telling anyone. If I thought this was bad then I would hate to know how much worse it could possibly be."

It was then that I saw how clearly Miss Bailoutte and Principal Hollerings and the Parents and School Committee and everyone in this entire bloody school had failed us. If they had done nothing and were still going to do nothing, then I was glad I didn't just sit there and wait for nothing to happen.

I could feel Jeremy Biggins' blood drying on my hand, and I didn't feel remorseful. I felt satisfied.

I took the drawing from Lexi, and that night at home, I burnt it.

eleven

I guess it's late. It's only a guess. I don't know anything anymore.

The doctor is pushing me hard, waiting for me to break.

But honey, I want to say, *you can't break something that is already broken.*

If he is going to be mean, then I am going to be meaner. I know there is only one way to play the game. After all, I was raised by my mother; *I am my mother.*

The doctor takes off his coat. He sits for a long time with his hands over his face. I watch him. I know he is tired; I am tired too. But I don't want to go back to my holding cell. I just want to sit here. Caught between two moments. I can't close my eyes. If I fall asleep now, I will either tip head-first into my nightmares, or I will wake up and find myself caught in them forever.

Eventually Dr Fadden lifts his head, sighs, and pushes his finger down on the record button.

"I said—"

"Be quiet, Eliza. I can understand what your mother goes through. You really are quite insufferable."

My mouth makes itself into an *O*. But nothing comes out.

"We are going to talk about the attack on Alistair Aardant. You will tell me how Neil Fernandes is involved in all of this."

"Neil is not involved in any of this."

"So it is just you and your friends then."

"Yes. Is that so hard to believe?"

Is it because we're girls? I want to say. *You think a bunch of girls are not capable of something like this?*

When I punched that little prat, Jeremy Biggins, I saw Aardant there in his face. And, for a moment, I had never felt like I was doing so much by doing something so meaningless. It was so simple. And suddenly I felt so much better. Especially when

I saw the blood. I wonder when Neil hit Aardant whether he saw a monster in there. I wonder if he saw my dad.

"You understand that I can't do much for you if what you did was premeditated," says Dr Fadden and he sweeps his hair back with his hand. "Give me something to work with Eliza. Tell me that you regret what you did."

"No," I say. "I don't. I'm sorry if his parents are upset, but I am not going to lie about it."

"Come on, Eliza. Tell me *something*."

"I can't."

"Then I can't do anything for you. Sorry."

Dr Fadden is so mean. He is so good at hurting my feelings.

"I'll make you a deal," I say. "You have to promise not to bring Neil into this, and I will talk."

"Eliza, it doesn't work like—"

"Yes! Yes, it does! You make it work. You said you weren't like all the shitty-touchy-feely others because you're an anthropologist! You're the man with the evidence. You make it work or I swear I will say nothing and you will have to jail me anyway. I mean it!"

I reach over and I turn the tape recorder off. Then I eject the tape, pull all the ribbon out of it and toss it aside.

"I mean it. I have never been so sure in my entire life."

◆❖

Principal Hollerings wanted to know what happened. I told him the truth. That I hated Jeremy Biggins and I wanted to punch him in the face, ever since I got the taste of karate chopping his hand all those months ago in History. Marianne said that she had asked me to do it. Lexi told him that she was the one that started the argument in the classroom. And you couldn't say that we lied.

Principal Hollerings asked if we had any regrets, and if there were any reasons that we could give him to help him understand. I said no. It was my choice alone. Principal Hollerings said in that case, since we gave Jeremy Biggins no rights, he was going to revoke our rights to the school motto. *See Yourself. Reward Yourself. Punish Yourself.* He was going to enact a traditional method of punishment.

Marianne was to be stripped of her duty as Ball Committee President. She would be given the chance to resign gracefully, or else she would be dismissed in front of her peers. Lexi was to be disqualified from being in the running to be Belle of the Ball. As for me, I couldn't be banned from the ball since my mother had already done that. I was to be given the thing I dreaded the most. I was going to be given canteen duty again. In the meantime, we were to be suspended for the rest of the year until the exams started.

When I was younger, I thought that if I ever did anything bad enough to warrant suspension, I would go out all guns blazing, like that movie *Butch Cassidy and The Sundance Kid* before it all turned sepia. I would walk out of school in front of all the other students while giving them a two-finger salute. But as Marianne, Lexi and I walked out those gates before it was even lunchtime, it was all deadly quiet. There wasn't anyone around. We got out of there as quickly as we could.

Marianne's parents were really angry. Even after they realised that they could do nothing about it, they couldn't stop telling her about their disappointment. Marianne said she just bowed her head and took it. She said it would have been worse if not for her parents' belief that she was going to be best in state and could still redeem herself. She once told me her greatest fear was not what her parents would do to punish her if she did something really wrong, but rather, how much less they would love her from that point on.

Lexi's father didn't say anything. Lexi stood there and told him what she had done and her father didn't utter a single word. When she finished and bit silently into her lip, apparently the only thing he did was nod. Then he left the room. Lexi's greatest fear is that she could never live up to her dead mother. She knows already she has as good as failed.

As for my own mother, she wasn't even there. She'd gone interstate again. Principal Hollerings tried to reach her on her mobile, but no one picked up.

"I'll be right looking after myself," I told him. "I've done it all my life." Principal Hollerings gave me a look that said he believed me.

When I got home I curled up on the shower floor and turned the water on hot. I sat like that for about an hour.

After my skin turned red and I felt like I was going to choke on my own rising vomit, I got out. The doorbell chimed. It was Lexi. She fell into my arms and I held her.

Marianne arrived about an hour later. Her parents had grounded her, but when has anything stopped Marianne?

"What can they do if I don't listen?" she said. "Punish me?"

We sat huddled around on the floor of my bedroom, barely talking, barely able to move. When it got dark we crawled into my mother's king-sized bed and we slept together like puppies.

The rest of the days in that week were pretty much the same. I don't remember much about them. Lexi and Marianne would appear at the front door before daylight. We tried to study, suspended in air-con. I would leave the house before midday to do my detention at the canteen. Emotionless and mechanical, I would serve the snotty juniors. Then I would come back and study some more. I shut my curtains so I didn't have to think of the water and the coast I could see from my bedroom window. Of hot sun and sweaty bodies and sunscreen lotion. Of blue skies.

◆❖

"Tell me when you came up with the plan?"

"Please don't call it that," I say to Dr Fadden. "It's not like we said to each other — *hey it's getting pretty boring, I know, let's go out and kill someone today, wouldn't that be fun?*"

"Then what do you call it?"

"I don't know."

Dr Fadden throws a folder at me. I jump.

"Coroner's report. Came back very interesting. Sounds like a plan to me."

"It wasn't."

"Then you explain it to me, Eliza, because I don't quite get it."

"I don't think you can."

Dr Fadden became quiet. He stretches his arm out and tilts my chin up with his finger. "Try me."

Damn that doctor.

◆❖

It started on the Monday morning. We were sitting around on the living room floor, trying to get ready for the first exam, the English Lit one that was on tomorrow. See what good girls we were?

"*Question 3: Different devices are used to develop the characters of protagonist and antagonist. Discuss this in relation to your reference novel. Or — 'Bad guys are better than good guys'. Discuss in relation to your reference novel,*" I read from the trial exam paper.

"What if a character is a *bad* good guy? Or a *good* bad guy?" asked Lexi. She rolled onto her stomach and chewed on the end of her pen. "That question sucks, I don't want either of the choices."

"That's too bad. It's a compulsory question. Choose part A or part B."

"It's a *trial* exam question. Not *the* exam question. I doubt we would get asked something as stupid that."

Lexi rolled onto her back and groaned loudly.

"I wish we could ask Mr Steele," I said and I sighed just as loudly to emphasise my point.

"Look, would you both like some cheese with your whine? I've heard nothing else since we've been here. I'm sick of it!"

We both stared at Marianne. This was the first time we had heard Marianne speak the whole morning.

"I'm sorry," said Lexi softly. "I'm sorry this is all my fault."

"Oh God, Lexi, you know I don't mean that." Marianne got up on her knees, dropping the papers in her lap onto the floor.

Marianne tried to crawl over to Lexi and touch her hair, but Lexi turned away.

"Look, if it makes you feel any better, I'm suffering too. I got fired from the Ball Committee — and suspended. It's not like I don't know how you are feeling—"

"Marianne, in case you forgot, I was disqualified from being Belle of the Ball and I am suspended too, for no reason! I thought I was the victim here, but obviously not! No! You have *no idea* what I am feeling!"

"I — I didn't mean that either," stammered Marianne.

"Then say something you do. If all those words that are

dribbling out of your mouth aren't what you mean, then just shut up."

"Come on Mari," I said and reached out a hand to touch her. "Let's just go and have a break in the kitchen—"

Marianne reeled. And then she turned on me.

"If you had never roped us into going to that stupid Jane Blonde party, then none of this would have happened!"

"What? I didn't make you go!"

"You were the ones who put our names down for it! Or do you not remember?"

"And what? I forced you into that attention-seeking dress you wore to make Gauntly notice you, did I?"

Marianne flushed red. Her mouth became a very straight line, but she was not done yet. Neither of us were. We were both standing and ready to go.

"You were the one who introduced Ellanoir Dashwood into our group! You changed something, Eliza — I knew she was bad news! I knew it from the start!"

"Oh! It wasn't that 'initiation' or whatever it was you took Ella and us on," I said angrily. "The one that impressed Jane Ayres so much she stole Ella from us! If that never happened then Jane Mutton wouldn't have punched Aardant in the face and made him bleed!"

"And who was it that put Aardant in that condition in the first place! *Your* friend, Neil!"

"Please! Just stop it!"

Lexi was between us, a hand on each of our shoulders.

"Don't say that, Marianne," said Lexi. "You know it isn't true. Neil is *your* friend too. He is *our* friend. And we don't have that many friends left."

Lexi bowed her head and looked at the ground.

"Don't fight. We're supposed to be closer than ever, aren't we?"

"Oh Lex," said Marianne. "How did it turn out like this?"

"Because it is Aardant's fault," I said glumly. "Come here."

I stretched my arms out and Marianne and Lexi both fell into me. We quivered together. Like quicksand. Unable to let go and unable to get out.

◆❖

It was me who suggested that we should pay Aardant back. I'd been thinking that maybe I did do something when I brought Ella into our group. It disturbed something that was fine before. I should try and make it better.

I had made too many excuses in my head — that Ella was new and didn't know anyone, that she was funny and smart. That she was too good for the Jane Blondes to have. Did I even like Ella as a person? I shouldn't have tried to mess with Fate. Ella ended up with Jane Ayres anyway. That is Fate.

I was thinking that if it really was my fault, if every reaction could be traced to an action before, then at the very beginning would be me at the canteen queue with my twenty-dollar note instead of my packed lunch. In turn I could blame my mother for not caring enough and maybe I could blame my father for making my mum stop caring. Maybe all this was supposed to happen. It had been happening all along. It was too hard to try and stop it now. In a twisted way, there was cold comfort in that.

Look at us. We had nothing left. Aardant *raped* one of us, and we were the ones stripped of every last thing we had. We were the ones punished. I thought again of that lifeless girl in the ditch. No one saw a thing. No one cared. And I was angry.

"We have to do something. I am sick of sitting around and waiting. I don't know what we are supposed to be waiting for anyway."

I stood up and I threw my books onto the ground.

"We either do something and suffer the consequences or we do nothing and let this destroy us. Which is what it's doing anyway. I don't know about you, but I've had enough. I am going to do something. Who's coming with me?"

Marianne and Lexi stared up at me in surprise.

In my head, I thought this would be incredibly difficult, but it was easy.

"Yup," said Marianne and she got up on her feet. Lexi did as well.

"No," I said. "I don't want Lexi involved in this—"

"Why?" asked Lexi. "Alistair started it. I will just end it for him."

There was nothing I could say in response to that.

❖❖

Brian, maybe you are right after all. It was a plan. It had a beginning, middle and an end. We knew what we wanted to do, what we were going to do, and how to do it. We never meant for it to turn out this way, but you're right. It was a plan. We got up off the floor and for the first time in two weeks, and we put our school uniforms on.

❖❖

Lexi was going to school to wait for Aardant, just before the last class was out. To say that she wanted to talk to him somewhere private. I didn't tell Lexi what to say. She's a smart girl; she'd know the right thing to do when the time came.

My uniform felt like a costume. I put on a fresh coat of black nail polish. I twisted up a tube of Revlon Red and put my war paint on. I sharpened the tips of my Fierce Words so they were like a row of shiny arrows.

I hitched Lexi's skirt up and tucked her phone into her blazer. *I will ping you when we're ready*, I said. *Then you take Aardant to the place.*

Her eyes were purple. Almost violet. Almost alien.

I went to wait by Ella's house. I knew from which direction she would be returning home from school. I had a few words I wanted to have with her. I didn't have to wait long before I saw her.

You know, it was a shame that Ella didn't stick with us as our second brunette. In the daylight, she made a really ugly blonde.

I approached her with my arms open like I was going to give her a big hug.

Come on, Ella, I said to her as she struggled with my embrace. *You're going to help us with a little something.*

She didn't want to go with me, but I didn't give her a choice. *This is like the good old times,* I said. *Don't you remember how much fun we used to have?*

I told her *we got into this mess together so now we were going to clean it up together.* It was going to be quality time; it was only right.

Down by the East Rivermoor billboard, Marianne was waiting. I went to stand by her, dragging Ella through the dust with me. The sun was high and shone hot on the scrub and the dirt. Beyond the ditch the old train bodies lay, rusty red with age and abuse. We waited. Soon we could see Lexi. She had Aardant with her.

◆❖

Okay, Brian, this is how it goes. Strap yourself in.

◆❖

Aardant saw us.

"What is this, bitch?" he said to Lexi. "What are your disgraced friends doing here?"

"This," replied Lexi and she pushed him. Caught off guard, Aardant stumbled and fell down in front of us. He was trying to get back up and was swearing at us, when I kicked him in the stomach. Then Marianne kicked him.

"How dare you think you can do this to us," Marianne screamed, and she spat on him. "How dare you think you can keep doing it and doing it!"

Marianne turned to Ella. "Go ahead, your turn." She pushed Ella forward.

"I don't want to," whined Ella.

"Don't be shy now! Make your new best friend Jane Ayres proud of you." Marianne grabbed the back of Ella's head. "Go on. Do something daring and maybe she'll be even more impressed this time."

"Okay, okay!"

So Ella kicked him too.

We watched Aardant squirming there on the ground.

"What — do you fucking want?"

"You admit what you did," said Marianne. "Look at what you've done. Look at her."

She brought Lexi over. Lexi looked so lovely. I believed when I looked into her eyes I could see the ruin inside of her. Her body was no longer her home; she could scrub what was left of her with him still on it until she bled, but she could not shed herself and step into a new skin. I couldn't believe that anyone could see her and be able to escape the guilt.

So I lost it.

"I hate you!" I screamed. "I hate you so fucking much! You tell her you're sorry — tell her!" I grabbed my own hair. "Are you still undecided about the colour? You really want to know if I can get angry enough to match it? Then you—"

"Fine! Fine!" said Aardant. "I'm sorry! I'm sorry!"

That made me stop dead in my tracks. Sorry wasn't a word I heard often. Especially not twice in a row. It sounded foreign. Like something for which my brain needed a translator. I was silent for a moment as I turned the words over like a pair of skipping stones.

I wasn't sure it was enough. I thought about taking off my shoe and using the heel as some sort of hammer, but a hand stopped my arm. It was Lexi.

No, she mouthed. *Go.*

I started at her. She nodded and I saw those eyes. Almost violet.

I turned away. I screamed in frustration. I took my shoe off anyway and threw it at his head.

"Good," said Marianne down to him. "I hope that teaches you a lesson. If you try to get any of us back, next time I swear, we will kill you. Come on girls, let's go. He's not worth anymore of our time."

That was true. The grand total of our entire plan. We were leaving. The problem was we were done with Aardant, but Aardant wasn't done with us.

The pride of Priory's football team threw his arm out and grabbed Lexi by the leg. She came crashing down. We all screamed at the same time. I could hear Ella's high-pitched scream above all of ours as she bolted away.

Fuck, I thought. I wanted to go after her and drag her back, but I turned, fell on my knees and grabbed Aardant instead.

I couldn't have anticipated what happened next. Aardant grabbed a switch knife out of his pocket. He put Lexi in a headlock and pulled her up against him, sticking the blade to her throat.

"Don't worry, babe. It's easier the second time," he said.

Tears welled up in Lexi's eyes and they brimmed over and spilled down her cheeks. Once was unforgivable. A second time was inconceivable.

I watched helpless as Aardant slowly dragged himself up, his arm around Lexi with the knife tight in his fist. At that moment I hated everything. I hated Priory. I hated East Rivermoor. I hated all the teachers and I hated the world and I hated everyone in it. I wanted to kill him or I wanted to die. There was no in-between.

Oh God, make this right, I prayed. *You owe me one, you really do. For all you have let happen, you owe me one.*

I threw myself at Aardant and I bit down on his shoulder. He let go of Lexi and Marianne pulled her away. I wrestled with Aardant to get the knife away from him. It was only when my fingers and the metal of the knife and everything I was touching started to feel slippery that I actually looked down. It was blood. I looked at Aardant. I dropped my hand away.

My mother's favourite artist is Alexander Calder. For her birthday many years ago, my father brought her a framed lithograph called *Sunburst*. She loves that lithograph so much it still hangs above her bed. Calder's *Sunburst* looks like a very violent, bloodied wound.

Right then Aardant had one of those blossoming on his white school shirt.

"Oh my God."

I didn't know what I had done. All I knew was that I was trying to get the knife away from him. Trying to stop him from hurting Lexi.

Later they would tell me that whoever stabbed him meant it as no accident. The knife was plunged in so hard it splintered one of his ribs.

'How does that feel!" Marianne was screaming. "Did you like that?"

"Shut up, bitch," Aardant said between gritted teeth.

"Just finish him off," demanded Marianne and she turned to me. "I am sick of him, just finish the bastard off, Lizzie."

I stared at Marianne, but I said nothing.

"Do it! He raped Lexi and he was just about to kill her! He probably would have killed you if you hadn't stabbed him instead. Do it!"

I felt the knife still in my hand. Still slippery with blood. I didn't know if it was all Aardant's blood or whether some of it was my blood as well.

"Mari, I do not take orders from you—"

It was the gunshot that made us all jump.

The next thing I knew, I was facing Lexi and she was covered in a fine mist of red. Then I realised that the wetness on me was the same thing. Like a summer shower. Only sticky and sweet.

Aardant groaned below us. His eyes opened really wide, then they glazed over and he was dead.

Omigod I'm gonna be sick. I put my hand over my mouth and squeezed my eyes shut. When I looked up again, there was Neil.

He took the gun that was in his hand and threw it into the ditch.

"Oh my God, Neil — why are you here?" I pressed my palms onto my forehead.

"Just passing by," replied Neil. "I was going down to the bridge."

"Don't give me that crap! What is this?"

"Okay. I followed you. Can you blame me? Do you know what happened here once?"

"Neil," I said. I could feel the tears prickling the corners of my eyes. "Neil, why did you do that?"

"We're friends, aren't we? Isn't this what friends do? Look out for each other?"

I didn't reply. But in my heart I said *yes*.

"This is for the best," said Neil. "He'll just get worse over time. He's a monster. Best to end it now. Trust me, *I* can tell."

Why should I trust you and what do you mean you can tell?
I wanted to ask him. *Aren't we all monsters? Including me?*
But I could feel my throat close up.

"Don't worry about anything, it's not your fault," he said.
"Just turn away from it. That's it — just look away. It's going
to be fine. Let me sort it out. Do you remember how you
trusted me with Rat B? Elle, will you trust me again?"

I nodded. What could I do? I did trust him. I trusted him
with my life.

Neil took me by the elbow and steered me away. I only
had one shoe. Where was my other…

"Girls, it's time for you to go home."

"Thank you, Neil," whispered Lexi, tears still streaming
silently down her face.

"Not a problem, Alex." Neil kissed her on the cheek.

"I'm glad you're our friend," said Marianne, as Neil
hugged and kissed her too. "I'm not sorry at all. I thought
I would be — but I'm not."

"Ah. Elle. Time for you to go home and get cleaned up."

Neil was staring at me. I realised that I probably had
smeared blood all over my face. I looked down at myself.
A patch of wet red was covering my heart, making my shirt
transparent.

"Why did you really do it?" I asked him.

"Are we going to speak the truth now?"

"Yes," I said.

"To protect you."

"You don't have to protect me."

"Of course I have to."

"I am not a weak little girl."

"Of course you are. The truth would crush you like the tiny flower you are."

I know I wanted to say, but I didn't want to cry in front of Neil.

"You don't give your mum enough credit for raising you, Elle. Look at you. Teenage sweetheart with a sugar shell and strychnine centre. We might as well finish speaking the truth now."

"It was my mum's fault—" I started to say.

"No, Elle," said Neil. "It was your father's. And my mother's. Your mother and my father were just the victims. You should try and understand that. Then you might start forgiving yourself."

I remembered playing *Hungry Hungry Hippo* on the floor with Neil. In his room with the plastic flying pig anchored on the ceiling. Going round and round in the heat of summer, buzzing like a blue bottle fly.

Oh God, why am I remembering this?

I asked Neil if I could go and find my father because there was something I wanted to ask him, or needed from him. I don't remember what it was anymore.

"He's not around," said six-year-old Neil. I left his

room anyway and I saw the light coming from Neil's parents' room.

"Look," I said to Neil and I pointed and smiled.

"No, not there," he replied and he led me gently away.

Why do I have to revisit these forgotten places?

◆❖

"Will you forgive yourself?" I whispered. I couldn't really talk anymore.

Neil didn't reply. He kissed me and wrapped his arms around me.

I wondered if I should have kissed him back. I wondered what that would have meant. If that would have changed anything. But the moment passed and it never happened, so it's no good thinking about it now.

"Let me have that."

I was still holding onto the knife. Neil took it from me and then he held it up to his face. He cut off a lock of his hair and dropped it into my palm.

"There you go, Delilah. I think this is what you wanted."

Later Marianne said: "I hope it rains and washes it away. That would bitch it up real good." But it never rained.

◆❖

I lay in my mother's bed that night, with Marianne and Lexi curled up next to me, thinking about Aardant's body. We left him where he was and we walked away.

I thought about Aardant and then the girl dead in the depths of that ditch, and I thought of Lexi and her warm, breathing body next to mine. *Oh God, I am so glad.* I grabbed Lexi's tousled head and kissed her hair. She smelt like John-Paul Gaultier and blood. Lexi mumbled noisily in her sleep and rolled over.

It took a while before it fully registered. Before it hit me that Neil had killed someone. All I had been thinking about was how he had saved us. How relieved I felt that he made a decision for me, one that I didn't know how to make myself.

I finally took the postcard out of my blazer jacket. The one with the picture of the assassination museum on the front. I put the lock of hair, tipped in Aardant's blood and folded it all up. Then I hid it where no one would find it again. It was not evidence. It was not going to be shown to the world. It was for me and me alone.

There was no way I could sleep for the rest of the night. I thought about how Neil knew exactly when to look up at me when I sent him those messages in my head during Politics. I thought about an unborn me and an unborn Neil connecting through our mother's bellies; floating like little spacemen, trying to grasp onto something, *anything*.

I pretended that I was a radar dish, opening up like a metal flower, tuning into *Frequency Neil*. Seeing if I could pick up any signals. If there were any I would find them.

Where are you right now, Neil?

Nothing. I didn't feel anything. I guess…maybe we were supposed to be just friends then.

◆❖

Now that I know how the story ends, I can see that Neil made sure to shut himself down, so that I couldn't see what he was doing. He had already left me a message, I just didn't know it. He had told me it was *going to be fine*. That he would *sort it out*. He said, *will you trust me?*

He gave me the answer when he was talking about things being over and about monsters being stopped. I thought he was talking about Aardant. When we found out the next day about Neil's suicide, it was then I realised that he was also talking about himself. He had said to me, *trust me, I can tell.*

◆❖

"I am done," I say to the doctor. "Take me back to my holding cell. I want to get some sleep. I'm exhausted."

◆❖

I sleep well that night. Maybe it does do you good to tell someone else your secrets. It's not only my truth — it is Lexi, Marianne and Neil's truth too. I just couldn't tell it earlier. I guess I wanted to show that we are people. That sometimes people can make horrible mistakes.

I don't think I can look at Dr Fadden again. I have opened myself to him. I am scared he is going to be able to look into my eyes now and see who I really am. A person I have been trying to hide all my life.

That's why when the door of the cell opens in the morning and he appears beside me to beg for more information, I don't want to talk to him. I roll over in my bed and face the wall.

"Eliza. Come on, Eliza. I know you don't want to sleep anymore. Talk to me."

"I have nothing more to say."

Marianne never got to sit the exams. No one will ever see her fresh and smiling face in the paper being proclaimed the state's top student. Explaining her handy study tips for next year's budding high-achievers and her plans for her very bright future. No one will ever believe that Lexi can be a role model to anyone. She won't be applying to do that volunteer year overseas in Laos.

As for me, I don't know. Maybe I lose nothing by not being special, after all.

"Thank you — for last night, but—"

Dr Fadden sounds excited. And desperate. I don't need that.

"I need you to help me, help yourself. Talk to me, Eliza."

"I just want to rest."

"Look, Eliza. I am going to be very blunt with you.

When this goes to court, you'll see how hard they come down on you. They'll tow a no tolerance line. You just watch."

"What can I do about that? I told you. I stabbed him. That's it."

"Eliza—"

I sit up on the bed and turn to face him. He's sitting there with his notebook on his knee.

"I know what they are on the cover of your little book. They're the Furies. The goddesses of vengeance. They're responsible for those that commit crimes against women and remained unpunished."

"They're not real," says Dr Fadden and his face darkens. He looks really fed up and tired. "I'll tell you what's real. I'm not here to try and defend you, I'm here to find the truth. I have it in my finding that the force of the stabbing would have been sufficient to kill Alistair Aardant if you had walked away and left him there. He would have suffered a very slow death, but he would have died. The question is, do you want to behave now, or do you want this to be told to the court?"

I shrug. "Let me tell you what I know about *you*. I think you ought to talk to your girlfriend Michelle, the one that gave you that notebook. She's wearing a pair of two thousand dollar designer heels. You should ask her who bought them for her, since it's not you, is it? Goodbye Brian. I hope you get a promotion. You deserve it."

"That's it?"

"Yes. 'Cos I want to see my mum now."

◆❖

They make me wait back in the interview room. I'm so bored. So I play a little game. I sit really still so that the only things that I move are my eyes. I roll them to either side of me and take in the painted brick walls. I roll them toward the ceiling and stare at the dark patch above me again. It looks like a black cloud. I could be a little cartoon sitting underneath it with a speech bubble that says, *Why does it only rain on me?* This is amusing and I smile.

Do you ever get so stressed sometimes that you go *uh-oh I think I've gone beyond it*, and then start feeling strangely calm? That's when I can really think. That's when I can actually see myself. Make-up, fake-up free, and sort of pretty. That's when the honesty comes.

I think about Richey Edwards from the band, Manic Street Preachers. One day he checked out of his London hotel and a week later his car was found parked near the Severn Bridge. He was never seen again.

Neil said we could rent a car. We'd have to get our licences first, but it would be okay 'cos they drive on the same side of the road as us; it would be like a reward for passing the first time. We could drive to the Embassy Hotel. Then we'll take the exact route to the bridge; we'll do Newport bus station, King's hotel, Blackwood — all the last sighting hotspots. Then finally we will stand on the bridge and look down. Neil will grab hold of my hand if it is windy. Otherwise I might blow away like a flower. When my hair gets tangled up by the wind this time, he reaches up and tucks it back behind my ear.

I'm playing the being really still game again. This time I roll my eyes toward the ceiling, not because it amuses me, but to keep the tears inside. But they come anyway.

If I was hiding myself in any way, I can't now. I have been stripped of whatever dignity I had and I am naked for the entire world to see. I am opening up like a flower. It is good to be open. Because honesty is a virtue. And the tears come.

◆❖

When my mother arrives, I try not to look at her. She is immaculately dressed in a black Armani suit and I don't want her to tell me that I look a mess and that I'm a disgrace to her reputation.

I didn't expect her to cradle my face in her palms and kiss me hard on the forehead.

"You're not wearing a skirt," I say cautiously, not wanting to let my defences down. I think about all the mean things I've ever said about her dress sense.

"Pantsuits are in this season," replies my mum and she self-consciously smoothes the fabric over her knees. "Let's get you out of here soon as possible, shall we?"

She doesn't mention anything about how I turned her away yesterday or the day before that. Inside I feel bad.

"Mum," I say. "I just want to tell you…thanks…for

taking care of me since Dad went. I just want you to know, that's all."

My mum stops unpacking her briefcase and she freezes. A tear rolls down her face and she quickly swipes it off her chin.

"What brought that on?" she says.

"I remembered what a really smart friend said to me once, and I reckon he's right."

There are only two ways out of East Rivermoor. Through the double gates or by the water, which takes you out to the ocean, eventually. Most of us never leave. The ones who do are the ones who choose to.

I wish I'd grabbed hold of his hand. It's always windy on that bridge. So he *wouldn't couldn't shouldn't* have gone.

Neil. I sorta kinda really need you. Needed you.

My mum pulls a face. Her mouth turns down, crows-feet gather around the corners of her eyes and a frown appears on her perfectly smooth forehead. Another tear falls down her face and it smudges her mascara. She suddenly looks so ugly. And yet she is the most beautiful I have ever seen her.

"I have something for you." She chokes on her words. From her carrier bag, she pulls out a flame-coloured dress and places it gently into my lap.

"Aurelio Costarella!" I exclaim and hold it up. I can't even remember the last time I saw decent clothes. I wonder if I can change into it straight away.

"It's your size, honey. It's a gift. In fact I can't stop them from sending stuff. But I guess you have to look nice for the media circus outside."

"Media circus?"

"You don't know? They've come to try and catch a glimpse of you."

My mum pushes something across the desk. It's one of those trashy women's magazines she buys religiously as soon as they hit the stands.

It's got the same stuff on the front as usual. So-and-so are still dating and what's-her-face apparently had another drug overdose. The only thing different about this issue is that it's got my mum right smack on the cover.

I read the headline. *Glamour Lawyer Speaks Out: My Daughter's Painful Murder Shame.*

I stare at my mum with my mouth open. I don't understand...I can't believe it. How could she? And so fast? The magazines must have really considered it the scoop of the century.

"You've gone national?" I ask in disbelief. I know she, like, makes the social pages in the *East Rivermoor Eye* all the time but...

◆❖

My name is Eliza Boans and I am a murderer. I *know*. It's pretty shocking huh? I want to grow up and do something cool with my life, such as build an orphanage in a third world country like a saintly Hollywood celebrity. That or, like, cause

a scandal and become mega-famous. Everyone knows that's
how you get noticed these days.

◆❖

I quickly flick the pages to check out the "exclusive six-page
photo spread". In the first photo my mum's leaning against
an outrageously hot male model and is wearing a red Ruth
Tarvydas dress slashed all the way to the thigh. She could pass
for a twenty year old. She looks…amazing.

"I *so* have to borrow this dress," I say.

"It's *so* not in your size. And you can't wear chicken fillets
in that honey, you actually need boobs," replies my mum and
she laughs and cries all at the same time.

"That's fine," I shrug and I laugh a little. "I'll just ask you
for a pair for my seventeenth birthday."

For the first time since I've been here, I smile for real.

It hurts to do so. I have pins and needles all through my
body, my brain and all inside my heart. The pinpricks are too
small to see, but I am bleeding, drop-by-drop. But I try to
think of all the good things. Like my new dress and my own
bed and my room and all my nice things. Nice things Mum
bought for *me*.

I guess it isn't that bad being Electra Boans' daughter.
My mum, come to think of it, is smart, beautiful, tough and
a survivor. Like me. I reckon we'll have a lot of things in
common to talk about when I get outta here.

In my head I can see the gates of East Rivermoor opening

as my mum and I walk through them together, hundreds of cameras around us going POP. I look to either side; there is Lexi and Marianne, and they run up to give me a hug.

I know it's not really about whether I can go back; it's about whether I *want* to go back. And that is hard. Right now I only want to think of the easy stuff. Like this beautiful dress sitting in my lap that I have been told is definitely mine — that is a nice, simple truth for me to hold onto.

In my head I can see the gates of East Rivermoor shut on me. But they say *this is not goodbye; this is just see you later.*

So I say, *see you for now.* I just don't know how soon is now. I sit in the middle and I wait.

Acknowledgements

Thank you to The Trinity — EeVon Loo (BetaGirl), Kim Wisniewski (CritterBoy and maker of Cups of Tea) and Olivia Osment (whom without, Priory would not exist). Melissa Keil (Editor Extraordinaire) who found me, and to Andrew Kelly, who took a chance on me.

About the author

Shirley Marr is an accountant by day and a masked writer by night. That's when she becomes her true self — Writer Woman, with her trusty sidekick, BetaGirl.

Despite being blasted for writing an avant-garde short story completely in dialogue in Year Eight, and being fired from the Yearbook committee in Year Twelve for being disruptive, she still loves to write things her way. This type of behaviour led her to be the only person she knows who has ever been kicked out of a bookstore. Shirley wishes to keep living this rock-and-roll lifestyle. *Fury* is her first novel.

Visit Shirley at: www.shirleymarr.net

"Once upon a time there was a girl called Scatterheart, who was selfish and vain, with a heart as fickle as the changing winds..."

Scatterheart
by Lili Wilkinson

Hannah Cheshire is rich and spoilt. She has servants to wait on her hand and foot — and Thomas, a passionate young tutor who fills her head with stories.

Then one day her father disappears, and she is left to fend for herself. Alone and penniless, she is sentenced to transportation for a crime she didn't commit.

Once Hannah considered Thomas beneath her: a servant, a commoner. Now she thinks of him more and more.

But will she ever see him again?

One girl's adventure to find happiness becomes a fairytale within a fairytale. A romantic story of power and love.

Hostage
by Karen Tayleur

The thing I remember is that the chemist floor had
a large black scuff near the counter.
I don't remember the knife.
I remember something cold on my neck, which could
have been a knife, or could just have been his long cold
fingers pressing in to me.
But it was the scuff I remember best.
I was thinking, 'Someone should really clean that.'
And then we were in the car.
And then we were gone.

Tully becomes a hostage when she is abducted
on Christmas Eve. Her ordeal lasts 24 hours.

Or so she says…

After
by Sue Lawson

What happens when you're not the cool kid at school anymore?

CJ has been banished to the country to live with his grandparents.
No one asks him if he wants to be there.
It seems like no one really cares.
And no matter how hard he tries to outrun it, trouble seems to follow him wherever he goes.

"This is a special book. Sue manages to weave the profound with the everyday language of a teenager."
— Jackie French

Sugar Sugar
by Carole Wilkinson

Jackie has left Australia with a psychedelic suitcase and a dream to become a world-famous fashion designer. She knows exactly where she's going and how she's going to get there. So how does a weekend in Paris send her spinning off-course? How does she end up somewhere she couldn't even find on a map?

"A beautifully paced, closely observed and utterly compelling story about losing a dream and finding your passion...you're not reading this book, you're living it."
— Julia Lawrinson